METATRONS' CHILDREN

WRITTEN BY CHY RYAN SPAIN
ILLUSTRATED BY SYDNEY KUHNE

Book Design: kd diamond

ISBN:

Published by Flamingo Rampant

www.flamingorampant.com

10 9 8 7 6 5 4 3 2 1

Printed in Korea

This book is dedicated to my ancestors, whose defiance allowed me to step into being. May their ferocity live on in our descendants.
- Chy

To Mother universe and all of the beautiful souls who support me and my big dreams, I am eternally grateful.
- Sydney

PROLOGUE

Whenever we would ask about the time before the Fall our parents would always answer in the same way. "There was no one big thing. All the little things just added up until one day ... we were here." They would make vague references to things we didn't always understand: Economic collapse. Environmental decay. Extinction events. Poverty, pandemic, patriarchy, white supremacy, capitalism. "People had a nice thing and ruined it" is all it really added up to they would say. "We try to live differently now."

Whenever we would ask "where did we come from?" Aba would say that it all began with one small group of the strangest individuals. Queer folks of every colour and presentation. Black and brown folks with practice in survival. Tough, talented people full of creativity and determination. Witches and warriors and teachers and outcasts – folks who didn't fit into the Old World after all and didn't mind so much that it was crumbling down around them. They were accustomed to building new communities. So at the moment where it seemed that no one would survive, they turned to face one another and they all made their way out to the middle of nowhere and started to get down to the business of creation.

Ama had an even more frustrating answer. That really we were from the stars. Every living thing of this world started out as a seed from the great sea of the Universe that somehow took root here.

The animals of the forest, even the trees themselves, were really cousins to us all. And so it was our duty to live in harmony with them. That was the mistake we'd made before.

Maybe one day, if it be the will of the Universe, we will all get to return to the stars.

"Your name is a gift
you can return
if it doesn't fit."

- Andrea Gibson

CHAPTER ONE

Yren raises a hand to shield their eyes from the scorching sun. From somewhere in the distance, Ama and Aba call out to them. Yren can feel the pain in their parents' voices. It terrifies; it pierces something deep within Yren's spirit to hear that sound. Their breath quickens; their stomach drops. At first Yren sees only flat, dry earth stretching out in all directions, and rippling waves of heat distorting the horizon. But squinting up their eyes, something new comes into focus – a gnarled, dead tree whose bare branches snake toward the sky. There; the voices are coming from there! Yren takes off sprinting toward the tree, the wind licking at their heels, the coarse sand flicking against their back.

There's electricity stirring in the air, a violent storm approaching. Behind Yren's left shoulder they can see the grey clouds billowing and the streaks of white-hot lightning dancing across the sky. A terrible booming thunder pushes its way over the Barrens, the rumbles pounding in Yren's rib cage.

The cliff's edge comes into view before Yren's brain can fully comprehend what it is. They slam both heels into the sand, but continue sliding forward, the muscles in their calves straining. The edge gets dangerously close; the sand gives way under Yren's feet. Yren grabs a limb of the dead tree to keep themself from falling into the ravine. The bark breaks the skin of their palms. The pain is sharp and sudden. A bit of blood mingles with the slick of sweat. But Yren is spared from falling.

From below Ama and Aba holler in agony, plead for help. Aba's leg is shattered. It's bent back at an unnatural angle and there's blood – so much blood – all over the ground beneath him. Yren tries to catch their breath. Ama's eyes are wide with fear, but her voice is loud, direct. She isn't strong enough to lift both herself and Aba up and out, she says. Yren is going to have to climb down to help. Ama yells up instructions and cautions. Get the rope from the satchel. Tie one end around the dead tree, and the other around your waist, Ama says. Yren's hands are shaky, and their fingers are slippery.

Just as Yren begins their descent they hear the sound. It's like the chattering the trees make when the wind whips through but ... heavier. It shakes the ground. It echoes off the curving slopes of the ravine. It puts fear in Ama's eyes.

Yren, stop! Don't come any closer, Ama yells. Yren opens their mouth to protest, but the giant wall of muddy water is already barrelling toward and over Ama and Aba. Gone! In an instant. Yren's parents staring up at them, begging for help one moment, and in the next: gone! Taken by the water. Rough water fills the ravine, high enough to splash Yren's ankles. Yren closes their eyes and clings to the rope. They start to lose their grip, their hands so very slippery. The edges of the ravine crumble away beneath the weight of the water, threatening to pull Yren under.

Yren darted upright from their sleep, sweating and panting. Three new moons had darkened the sky since Ama and Aba had gone and Yren was still having nightmares about their disappearance. Unti said it was to be expected, called it "reliving a traumatic incident." Adults always seemed to save the fancy words for the most terrible things. Yren didn't care much for fancy words. They just wanted to stop dreaming about the death of their parents.

CHAPTER TWO

"Again?" A wry voice droned from the corner of the cabin. Yren swiveled to see the face of their sib, Augi.

"None of your business," Yren huffed, still struggling to catch their breath.

Augi's tone shifted immediately. "I'm only teasing. I'm sorry."

"Don't bother. It's fine." Yren caught Augi's worried glance and shook it off. "Really, Augi."

Augi was a little less than two years younger than Yren and when they were little they had been virtually inseparable. Perhaps it just took time for them to grow into their differences?

"Like bookends, those two," Aba would chuckle. "Night and day."

This sentiment was echoed in the siblings' somewhat shocking appearance. Yren's complexion was dark, luminous, and their hair a billowing mass of thick wooly coils. Augi had an almost lavender cast to his pale, pink skin. His tight curly hair, brows, and lashes were a fine, ashy blond. Other than that Yren and Augi's features were practically identical, so much so that it was undeniable the two were siblings. "Like some sort of bizarre mirror." Yren managed to overhear all sorts of things they'd rather not have heard, from adults mostly. Though folks were always kind enough, even as a young child Yren could sense how people gawked at the two of them as they ran, playing through the trees or up and down the Village paths. People were warm, sometimes even overly friendly, but they noticed.

It never seemed to bother Augi.

Radiating joy was Augi's protection. He laughed the loudest, danced the hardest, and seemed to find pleasure in everything life had to offer. There was an ease in his presence. Augi simply loved his life so much that he made it easy for people to love Augi as well. He was a bright, inquisitive child – always asking questions, always joking and causing mischief.

Yren — the elder — was aloof, brooding, and mistrustful of virtually everyone. Possessed by a quiet, roiling anger that lay just beneath the surface of their calm, detached exterior. "Sensitive" was the kindest way to say it. "Moody" would be more apt. Yren just felt their feelings deeply. More than that, they seemed to feel other people's feelings as well. They soaked up what didn't belong to them. Empathic. Ama had tried to encourage Yren's overwhelmingly compassionate nature, their wildly observant mind. It just made Yren ever more hyper-aware of being different from most of the people around them. It had only gotten worse when Yren first took ill.

Yren slipped out from under the bedclothes and stumbled over to the basin in the common room to splash a few handfuls of water over their face. The floorboards of the cabin were cool beneath Yren's bare feet, despite the heat outside from the midsummer sun. It was somewhat comforting to have the earth hold firm under their weight as they recovered from that lingering feeling of falling in their dream. Yren took several deep breaths and started to ground themselves with the game Ama had taught them: five things you can see; four things you can touch; three things you can hear; two things you can smell; one thing you can taste...

Yren looked around. Yren's tether danced midair just above their right shoulder. Its translucent body diffused the light, and its feathery limbs beat a soft rhythm against the air. The walls of the cabin Yren's ancestors had built nearly a hundred years ago ran in long, perpendicular lines to a huge stone hearth, though there was no need for a fire in this heat. Yren's eyes lingered a bit too long for Augi's comfort on a bright rectangle of afternoon sun streaming through the open shutters.

"Are you still here?" Augi chuckled. "You forgot, didn't you?"

Yren had meant to only take a short nap as a break from their chores. Yren had spent the earlier, cooler hours of the morning gathering water from the cistern to replenish the basin in the cabin. It was heavy, awkward work, hauling buckets of water from the cistern and back. Then they had stripped all the beds to wash the bedclothes and hung them out of the line to dry. By the time Yren had got around to putting fresh sheets on the beds it was midday. The heat of the day had simply drained them, and their bed was cool and inviting. Yren hadn't meant to sleep quite so long; they were disoriented and more tired than they had been when they had gone to lay down in the first place.

"Jedda's Naming Day. I haven't forgotten. Is it time?"

"Unti sent me to get you. They've started."

"I'm ready. Let's go."

"For a second I thought you were missing it on purpose."

"No matter how much I can't stand Jedda Quay, you know I wouldn't miss a feast. That family has been preparing for this all year. I bet there'll be all sorts of yummies." Yren shot a sideways glance at Augi and they both roared with laughter.

"Come on, then. Let's get you something to eat!"

Yren and Augi left their family cabin and took a shortcut through the light brush rather than along the dirt path. Yren wanted a view of the water. They wound around the perimeter of the

lake to watch the sun begin to set. It had been such a gorgeous day and Yren craved a little sliver of peace before the party. Loons called back and forth to one another in the distance, their cries echoing through the wilderness. A steady breeze rustled the limbs of the maple, pine, birch, and spruce trees that dominated the landscape. Falling acorns knocked against the trunks of trees as they skittered to the ground, and red squirrels chittered gleefully.

Augi sighed, shielding his eyes from the light reflecting off the water. "We're so lucky to live here."

"Augi, we're lucky to be alive at all."

"There you go again. Doomsayer."

Yren flinched. They agreed with their sibling, they were very fortunate to be able to call this land home. Somehow this forgotten expanse of wilderness endured even as the rest of the world had all but burned down. Yren knew how lucky they were, and yet they were still so sad.

"I miss Ama and Aba."

"Yeah. Me too." Augi reached for his sib's hand. "We have each other. And we have Unti. And what did Ama always say?"

"There is Blood and there is Family. One you are given and the other is a choice."

"We get to choose our family, Yren. I choose you."

CHAPTER THREE

In the months since the accident Augi had become increasingly kind to his sibling. It was awkward. Yren often didn't know what to do with such kindness. Yren had not expected to be so angry, to feel so betrayed by the *Loving Spirit of the Universe*. Those were the words that Ama used when she prayed. Lately, when Yren spoke to the Universe there were acid words and bitterness. A *loving* spirit wouldn't have taken Ama and Aba away, not like this. Yren had no prayers left, only curses. Sometimes Yren caught themselves thinking: *It should have been me instead. This is my fault.* Sometimes Yren wondered if they would ever pray again, if they could even remember how.

Yren had listened to Ama pray often as Yren had lain in bed feverish, exhausted, and afraid. Their isolated village had managed to avoid the Plague for decades but one day, somehow, the virus that had already taken so many others had found its way into little Yren's lungs. Everyone thought that surely they would all die, it was only a matter of time. It was then that the tethers had first arrived.

Yren and Augi had never been to the ocean, their home was too far inland, but Aba spoke of creatures that lived in the sea called "jellyfish" – clear globs of snot-like goop with ropes of poisonous stingers dangling from their bodies. They sounded disgustingly awful, and nothing like a tether. Still, Aba said tethers reminded him of jellyfish. This impression, coupled with the fact that no one had ever seen anything quite like a tether before, led them all to be deeply unnerved the morning they first saw the tether hovering over Yren's sickbed. Aba's first instinct had been to kill it. Thankfully, Ama had stopped him when she saw Yren's eyes bright and alive, and Yren's lanky, six-year-old arms reaching up to caress the tiny creature floating just above. Yren had seemingly made a full recovery. Ama said it was nothing short of a miracle.

Many of those afflicted had succumbed to the Plague and died, so word of Yren's recovery spread quickly among the People of the Village. Those who still lay consumed with fever, were visited by these otherworldly creatures. At first they were thought to be parasitic, something more akin to a leech. Rather than feeding on the blood of their hosts, these creatures seemed to feed on the virus itself. Seeing that Yren had been cured – and so quickly – the decision was made by the Council to allow the tethers to claim their hosts. Those who cared for the sick watched hopefully as the tethers set about their strange work.

Not everyone survived. Sadly, for most it was too late. It was discovered that if the tether could not reverse the virus, it would waste away with its host. The strange, translucent creatures disintegrated and absorbed into the body of their dying patient. Was this a final act of sacrifice, an attempt to nourish the body of the dying with their own life? There was something more going on here than had initially been thought. The tethers did not appear to be parasitic at all. They didn't diminish life, they didn't take from their hosts without giving.

For those the tethers were able to cure, not only was the illness removed, but the well-being of the person to which they were tied was amplified. People felt stronger than they had been before becoming sick! And after a few weeks the tether simply flitted away, like something out of a dream.

For a handful of those cured, something even more fantastic occurred. Some tethers remained long after their hosts were healed, and the people these creatures tied themselves to gained other benefits. They were exceptionally strong, or exceptionally fast. They could hear things from a great distance or see further and more clearly. They bonded more deeply to the animals in their care and those animals, in turn, seemed to follow their command. These little, otherworldly beings tied themselves to a person, and then seemed to tie that person to life itself. It was how they came to be called tethers. However, even these tethers eventually left their hosts behind, though the gifts they had bestowed remained. Six years later, it was only Yren's tether that maintained its connection to its host. All of the others had ascended back into the night sky from where they had come.

Standing there by the lakeside, the sun setting before them, Yren's tether danced down the length of their arm and came to rest on Yren and Augi's clasped hands. Its feathery tentacles pulsating and tickling them both gently as if it too wanted to hold hands. Yren and Augi giggled and then let go of one another.

"Hungry?"

"You bet."

CHAPTER FOUR

All fifteen of the Village families gathered in the Longhouse to celebrate the Naming Day of Jedda Quay.

Set back a ways from the rocky lakeshore, the Village Longhouse stretched across a mossy clearing between the water and the woods. Fog rolled off the lake in the cooling twilight and mingled with the smoke of the cooking fires so that the Longhouse lay veiled by a thin haze. Its massive steel ribs rippled through the mist and Yren imagined as they approached that it was the skeleton of some giant beast. The warm glow of firelight and the scent of roasting meat emanated from the structure. The sounds of distant laughter and drumming reached out to them.

The Longhouse was an innovative bit of engineering consisting of two massive, modified, forty-foot-long steel shipping containers, stacked one atop the other. Running the length of the perimeter was a platform of wooden decking, covered in part by sheets of corrugated galvanized steel. Solar panels sprouted from the roof in neat rows, powering batteries tucked away safely inside.

Like the traditional caretakers of this land who built longhouses before them, this longhouse was used by the People of the Village to store preserved food and firewood, and to gather together for ceremonies and celebrations. The Fifteen Families would collectively bunk inside the Longhouse during harsh winters, rather than freeze in their separate single-family cottages. Should there ever be an attack on their settlement, it would be to the Longhouse they would all go to barricade and defend themselves.

"You're late, Yren Stone!"

Yren had barely crossed the threshold of the huge, open steel

doors to the Longhouse when Jedda pounced, grabbing Yren's side in a swift, aggressive tickle. Yren glared back incredulously. Jedda was always touching Yren without asking.

"Well, I didn't want to come." Behind Yren, Augi muffled his laughter with his hands.

"Cute. But you don't fool me," Jedda giggled. "Come dance!"

"Maybe later, Jedda."

"Suit yourself," Jedda chirped back haughtily. "August?" Jedda extended her hand and Augi took it reluctantly. As he was dragged into the dancing crowd he shot a look back at his sibling as if to say you owe me.

Yren stood near the doorway and took in the energy of the space. The walls and ceiling of the metal structure were festooned with brightly coloured cloth banners. Through the open steel doors to Yren's right wafted the most alluring scents. The cooking fires were set up just beyond, and though they couldn't see the blaze they could certainly taste the flavours in the air. Yren's mouth watered, imagining the racks of roasting venison and goose, the heaps of crisp fruit and field greens. Wave upon wave of joyful noise washed over Yren's entire being. In the far corner of the room, on a slightly raised platform, seven drummers beat out a celebratory rhythm. Yren admired their swollen, calloused hands, their broad smiles. Yren considered the tremendous effort it must take to maintain such a steady syncopated pounding. But the drummers appeared invigorated, fortified by the beat they were creating together. This energy, in turn, electrified the crowd around them. The People danced, their brown bodies pulsing and swaying in conversation with the rhythm that echoed off the steel walls of the Longhouse.

"Yren, I made a plate for you." The gentle rumble of Unti's

deep baritone voice cut through the din of the music. He sat just off to the right in a quiet corner of the room on a pile of cushions, smiling at Yren knowingly. Unti had dressed for the occasion. His thick, salt-and-pepper locs hung down his back in an elegant braid. He wore several rings of silver on his broad, brown hands. He had shaped his beard and traded in his usual muddied working attire for a linen tunic and matching drawstring trousers of rich, saffron yellow. Even more beautiful was the magnificent array of roasted venison, squab, corn, and root vegetables that sat atop a low table in front of Unti. Yren quickly washed their hands in a shallow basin of water just beside the table before selecting a few savoury morsels with their fingers. Unti chuckled. "How was your day, little one?"

Between bites Yren squeaked out a "fine" and kept on eating.

Unti shook his head lovingly at his nibbling. "You should come up for air every now and again, okay?"

Yren shot a smile back. "Sorry. How was your day?"

Unti sighed a bit and turned his face toward the party as he answered. "I spent it helping to prepare for this evening." His wistful eyes took in the dancing crowd as he continued. "You'll be next, you know."

"I know. I wish Ama and Aba could be there to see it."

Unti turned swiftly back toward Yren. "Me too." They were both silent for a short while after that.

"Yren, your mother and father were very proud of the person you've become. You know that, don't you?"

"I guess."

"Your father and I were about your age when I first figured out that I was gay. He was the first person I told; did I ever tell you that?"

"No. But he did," Yren giggled a little.

Unti raised an eyebrow, "I see. And why do you think he would tell you something like that?"

They thought earnestly for a moment and then replied. "To let me know that it was okay to be different. To let me know that it would be alright if I ..." Yren's words trailed off.

"Your father was a good brother, a good person. He loved and accepted me just as I am no matter what, and it meant the world to me to know that he had my back. Sometimes all it really takes is one special person like that to get you through a lifetime of troubles. I see a lot of me and him in you and Augi."

Yren liked it when Unti talked like this. It was gratifying to be able to see their family's story from someone else's perspective.

"And the Village is a good place, Yren. These people are good people. Strong, fierce, loving people. You're safe here. You can feel whatever it is you need to feel. You can be whatever it is you need to be. You can speak yourself into this world – the same way Jedda is about to do – and know that we, all of us, will have your back. Understand?"

Yren nodded. "Yes, Unti Alton."

Augi plopped down in the space next to Yren, panting and sweating and smiling broadly. He caught the somewhat solemn glances going around the table as he washed his own hands in the basin. "Is the Doomsayer at it again, Unti?"

"All my fault, Augi. I'm being far too serious for the occasion."

"Uh, yeah!" Augi's face twinkled in the dim light of the lamps. His cheerful demeanor once again chasing away all traces of gloom with nothing but the brightness of his presence. He scooped up a few mouthfuls of food with his hands and looked around the room, taking in the music and the chatter around them.

Yren considered Unti's words further. The Longhouse was indeed full of people Yren admired and respected. There was Elder Jean Lemieux sitting across the way. Elder Jean's people were descendants of the Huron Wendat, the original caretakers of this land. He'd been born in 2048 and it stretched Yren's imagination to its limits to think about what life must have been like back then. Elder Jean had also had the plague when Yren was a small child, and it frightened everyone in the Village terribly to picture their lives without his guidance. He and his family had been an integral part of helping the Village to thrive, directing their practices to be in harmony with the land. They had shared knowledge on the patterns of the fish, birds, and animals so that the People could hunt sustainably. They had taught the People how to not overwork the land, which crops to plant where and when, what trees to clear and in what measure, so that their home remained fertile and thriving. Thankfully, a tether found its way to Elder Jean Lemieux's bedside to nurse him through his fever, and to connect him with Story. Dogs were few and far between in this New World, but wolves began to flourish in the wild. As a pup, Story found himself a place curled up at the foot of Elder Jean's bed and even after the tether was gone, Story remained. Despite his intimidating size and massive teeth, Story was just about the sweetest creature one could ever hope to meet. Their bond was a special one, Story and Jean. It made a person believe in magic just to look at the two of them together.

In the middle of the dance floor, creating an absolute riptide of gaiety was little Oscar Venegas. They had just turned fifteen, but Oscar was barely five feet tall. Still, they were one of the biggest personalities among the People. It was hard to imagine that only a few short years ago, Oscar had been such a sullen, shy child. That was before their Naming Day, before Oscar was Oscar. It gave Yren a thrill to watch another person blossom like that, to step into their place among the People with so much pride, certainty, and purpose. Yren watched as Oscar danced their way between Augi and Jedda Quay, and then out past open steel doors to catch their breath in the fresh air.

Yren's gaze drifted some more until it landed on Jedda's mother, Nyx Quay, proudly watching the party from the edge of the dancing crowd. Nyx Quay kept her head shaved down close to the scalp in the summer and all her shirts had no sleeves. Her arms and legs were ropes of thick muscle and she liked to show off the tattoos that adorned them. She had a booming laugh that both startled and delighted, and she was kind and fair, though she didn't always smile easily. One of the very best trackers in the Village, Nyx took the lead of just about every successful hunt.

To Nyx's left sat Jedda's other mother, Stokely. Like Yren's own mother, Stokely had a deep knowledge of the movements of the planets and the stars, and an enduring memory for the habits of the animals. If a person in the Village was confused about a certain course of action, or required a healing poultice or potion, they went straight away to seek her council. When a baby's arrival was imminent, Stokely came to the birthing person's aid. Aba had once told Yren that men in the Old World often mistrusted or even feared women like Stokely Quay. He said, "Witches, augurs, midwives, cunning women... these were just names for people who understood things that others couldn't or called upon powers most folks ignored or shut down in themselves." Among the People, Stokely was an excellent teacher and shared her gifts and knowledge liberally.

It was a marvel how two such lovely people, whom Yren idolized, could be responsible for that brat Jedda Quay. Jedda was a bully and a liar. She was talented and intelligent, but egotistical and more than a little cruel. She often picked on the weaker or younger children. She often made up stories to win this one's favour, to gain that one's praise, or to diminish someone else's achievements. What was worse is that Jedda actually liked Yren. For some strange reason she had decided that Yren was actually worthy of her respect. "I think she might actually have a crush on you," Aba imparted to Yren one day. "Maybe try being a little nicer to her and see if that changes things." So Yren had tried that for a time, but it only encouraged more of the same behaviour from Jedda. Yren now found her absolutely insufferable.

"Unti Alton," Augi chirped excitedly.

"Yes, my love."

"Why do we have Naming Days?"

Yren watched the expression on Unti's face warm. "Well, my love ... as you know, a Naming Day ceremony takes place on a person's thirteenth birthday. That is when it is time for a person to start moving out of their childhood and into their place as an adult among the People. Now, as adults among the People, we try to manifest our authentic selves in everything we do. In order to do that, we have to name ourselves into being."

Augi's face softened into a look of enthralled confusion. Yren chuckled to see their sib so consumed by Unti's words.

"The names we are given as infants are a gift, and not all gifts suit the person to whom they are given. Just like clothing, some names fit poorly or don't match our sense of ourselves. Some names chafe, they irritate our skin. We dislike the colour or the pattern some names cast us in. Some names we simply outgrow. So it is too with our pronouns – the words we use to refer to someone when we aren't using their proper names – words like she, her, hers, his, or theirs."

"You mean like how people say both he and they when speaking about you, Unti?" Augi asked.

"That's right, Augi. Even the name you use for me, Unti, is just a clever way of saying both auntie and uncle in the same breath. It is a way for the people who love me to honour all the parts of me, a way for me to feel seen, respected, and appreciated. And you're my nibblings – the children of my sibling – rather than using words like niece or nephew. So that you feel seen, respected, and appreciated no matter who you become."

"In the Old World people often had to hide their true selves in order to be safe, or to feel loved and accepted. Some people went a lifetime pretending to be someone they were not, allowing those around them to call them by a name that didn't fit them. And so, we found it useful among the People, to have a day for everyone to be celebrated for exactly who they are. To stand before the Village and name themselves into being. To either keep the gifts that they were given at birth, or lovingly decline them and instead claim what name fits them best."

"Asé," whispered Yren.

"Blessed be," added Unti.

"Attention please, everyone! Attention!" Nyx Quay called out to the assembled. "It is time."

The people of the Village made their way out of the rooms of the Longhouse and toward the rocky lakeshore nearby. There a massive fire pit stood, ablaze. It was surrounded by dozens of

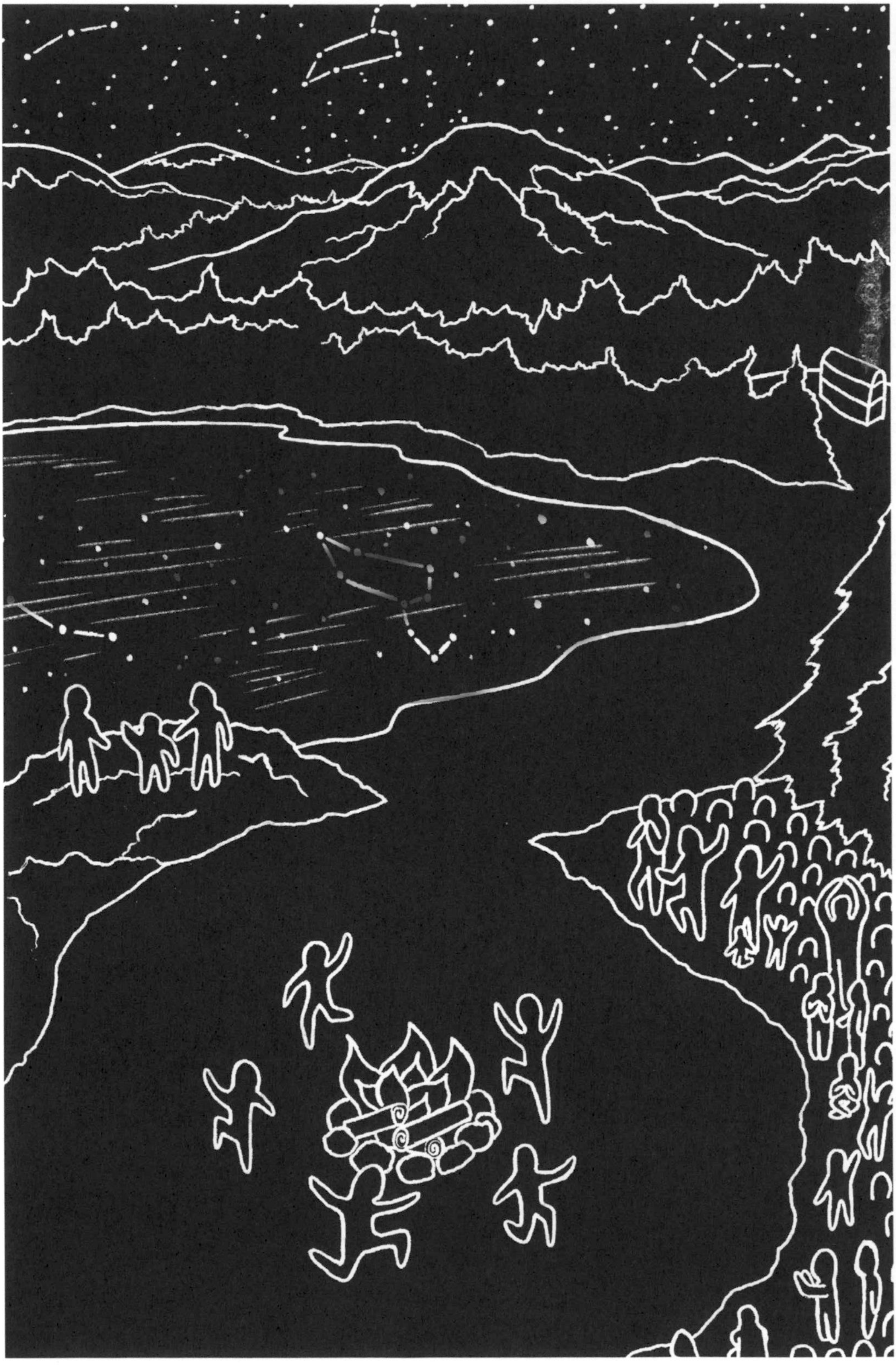

smooth paving stones arranged in a circle and raised shelves of seating composed of similar stone, creating a small ceremonial amphitheatre. The people sat along the rocky outcropping as Jedda, Nyx, and Stokely took their place in the centre, closest to the roaring fire.

"Leo shines above us in the heavens," Stokely called out, one finger pointing straight upwards into the night sky "as it did on this day thirteen years ago, when we welcomed this child into the arms of the People." Stokely placed a hand on Jedda's shoulder and smiled just as Nyx did the same from Jedda's left side.

Stokely continued the ritual. "The Universe is Love. Love is where your name is safe in the mouths of others. A name is a spell, a prayer. There is power in a name. They remind us that we are all a part of the Divine, who is all things – male, female, both and neither. The words we choose have power. What words do we use for you when we do not use your name? How Do We Call You?"

The words came strong and clear from the mouths of every person assembled at the water's edge. Their collective call echoed off the stone circle and bounced into the wilderness. "How Do We Call You?"

"I am Jedda Quay. You may call me She. Her. Hers. I choose the path of Hunter."

Nyx threw her head back and howled into the night. Story joined in for good measure. The drummers began a joyful rhythm and the Village erupted in dance and celebration.

Unti Alton leaned over to Augi in the seat beside him and whispered softly to him. "Jedda will become an apprentice with the hunters now. She will learn how to honour the spirits of the animals who feed us, how to fight and defend the People. When your turn comes, you can choose whatever path best fits you. We are not all born to fight. Some of us are farmers, or makers, or musicians, or healers, or teachers. You'll be drawn to your calling, and you'll find your place among the People when it is time." Unti looked back and forth between Yren and Augi with pride. "The two of you are meant for great things. I trust it."

Yren smiled shyly at their loving guardian, their father's sibling. Unti hugged each of them closely, sweetly, before running off to join the dancing.

Augi stood and looked back at Yren, his hand outstretched. "Coming?"

They were lucky to be alive, lucky to be among the People. It felt wrong to go on enjoying life with Ama and Aba gone, but at this moment it felt even more wrong to not enjoy life. "Yes," said Yren as they took their sib's hand. Augi pulled Yren into the dancing crowd. There Yren's sorrows slowly faded away as they found themselves moving to the pounding drums of their people, in the fire's light by the water's edge under the twinkling stars of the night sky.

CHAPTER FIVE

Surrounded by a fog so thick that it is only possible to see a few metres in any one direction, Yren stands alone in a dense forest of trees. Yren wants to panic. Yren wants to run, but to rush would be foolish. In this fog, at high speed, Yren would inevitably run right into the trees. It simply cannot be avoided. The best way to move forward safely is to let the trunks be a guide rather than an obstacle. Yren extends a hand and lets it come to rest on the trunk of a tree, then edges their feet forward slowly until another tree comes into view. Once a tree is behind them, it can support Yren's weight. Yren can let go of the tree behind them when they have managed to place the other hand firmly on the next tree in front of them. In this way, bit by bit, they make progress. It feels silly, the need to be in constant contact with something, but it makes Yren less fearful. To have one hand on the tree behind is reassuring. Without it Yren feels very certain they would be lost, alone. Besides which, the alternative – to not move – is terrifying: to be stood still, not knowing where they are or where they are going. Yren can hear the piles of dried pine needles crunching beneath their feet. Forward is the only option. The only way out is through.

Still a bit groggy and rubbing the sleep from their eyes, Yren lay there and stared at the cabin ceiling. It was still quite dark. The sun had only just started to climb, but the birds had already begun to sing.

Yren's tether flitted into view. It swirled above in easy, fluid movements, its thread-like limbs trailing behind the rest of its translucent body. It cooed softly, almost imperceptibly, as if to say "Good morning." Still languishing in bed, Yren extended a hand and the tether nuzzled into Yren's outstretched palm. It wrapped its arms around Yren's fingers and vibrated pleasantly. Yren giggled and smiled.

Yren sat up in bed, and the tether contracted its warm, smooth body into something almost snake-like. It spiralled around Yren's arm, still purring happily. In this form it climbed Yren's body up to the shoulder, and then unfurled again behind Yren's right ear, as thin and as flat as a pancake. It cradled the back of Yren's head and neck in its tendrils and disappeared in the nest of Yren's giant, wooly hair. It liked to sleep there; it felt safe and warm. If Yren did nothing to disturb or startle it, there it would remain for the bulk of the morning, sleeping peacefully.

"I don't know what you get up to in the middle of the night that makes you so sleepy in the day."

Indeed, Yren did not know much about the curious little creature curled up and sleeping in their hair. Of course the people of the Village had speculated, but no one knew for certain.

Scientists thought that the octopus had come to live in the Earth's oceans from another world because it was so genetically dissimilar to anything else on the planet. Some even went so far as to say that the building blocks of all life on Earth had rained down from the cosmic tails of comets billions of years ago. On a long enough timeline, maybe everyone was alien in one way or another. It was fun to think that perhaps the tethers weren't of this world at all, but little aliens. Then again, so many of the creatures of the Earth had gone extinct, who could say if something new hadn't emerged or evolved in that time to take their place?

It had never occurred to Yren to be afraid of their tether. As strange a thing as it was, they had never felt a moment of fear or apprehension toward it. For days Yren had lay in bed, feverish and woozy, drifting in and out of sleep. The tether had rescued Yren from one the most terrifying experiences of Yren's life.

Ama and Aba had been worrying over Yren day and night,

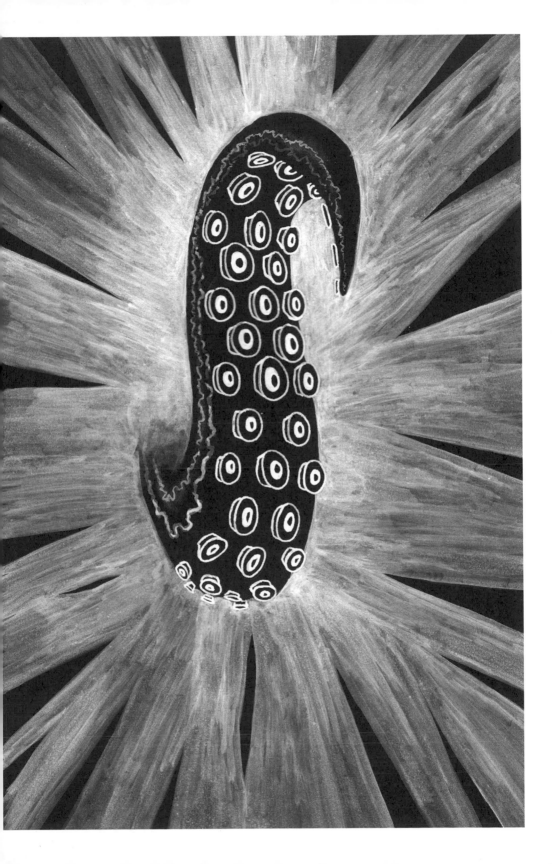

sleeping in shifts to care for Yren. It was the worry in their faces that had really frightened Yren. It scared them more than their own pain. It was only from the look in their parents' faces that Yren understood just how sick they were, how close to death.

Aba had been asleep in a chair at Yren's bedside when the tether had first arrived in the middle of the night, lilting through the open window. Yren had been half asleep themselves but had awoken because of the light. Light like moonlight was pouring into the cabin. Had it been a full moon? Yren had a vague memory of the creature hovering above their bed in a beam of soft, cold light. The being had danced just out of their reach, gliding through the air like water. Yren had been delirious with fever for days. They remembered thinking it was all some sort of dream. The tether hummed, and it purred, and it came closer and began to massage Yren's body with its own. The relief had been almost instant, the pain just seemed to melt away. Yren had relaxed into the feeling and drifted back into sleep.

The next morning, Yren awoke to find Aba screaming a short distance off with an axe in his hands. Ama was holding him back from charging towards Yren's bed. Yren had leapt up from the sheets and backed up against the cabin wall, in shock and horror, terrified. Tears streamed down Yren's face.

"Baby?" Ama stared at Yren, mouth agape. "Baby? You're okay! You're okay!"

"Don't hurt us!" Yren shrieked.

Aba dropped the axe to the ground and edged slowly toward his child.

"Yren, baby. Don't move."

"Stay back! Don't hurt us!"

"Honey ... no, no." Ama's voice was a defeated, heartbreaking whisper. "Aba isn't trying to hurt you, baby." Here Ama and Aba exchanged cautious glances. In a calm and quiet tone that couldn't quite mask her own panic Ama said, "There's ... *something* ... on your arm."

The tether was wrapped around Yren's left arm, vibrating swiftly.

"Here to help us," Yren heard the words coming from their own mouth. "No fear." Yren was dizzy, overwhelmed with exhaustion. After so many days of high fever and little food all of this sudden activity was too much. "No ..."

Yren's body went limp and they slumped against the back of the cabin wall. Aba swooped in and scooped Yren up in his arms. They carried Yren back to bed and Ama had kept a careful watch over her child for the next few hours while Aba had rushed out to alert the Village Council.

CHAPTER SIX

"Shouldn't you be in school?"

Yren had reached the edge of town where Elder Jean Lemieux had set up his trailer. There he sat in his grand old rocking chair with a blanket thrown over his legs and his cap pulled down over his eyes. At first Yren wondered how he had even noticed them passing, but then saw Story standing guard a few metres off. Elder Jean took a thin branch and poked around a small fire pit from the comfort of his seat. He had a kettle brewing and a pot of beans stewing. Yren couldn't quite see his eyes but could sure make out that grin.

Yren had washed and got dressed in the semi-darkness, being careful not to wake Unti or Augi. Last night's celebration had run long. Certainly some folks had just gone to bed a few short hours ago, and a good portion of the Village would still be asleep now. Yren had opted to leave the festivities a bit early. Jedda had proved overly persistent in attempting to get Yren up to dance. At one point Yren literally took hold of Augi, thrust him between them and Jedda, then took off for the quiet of the woods.

Yren had a quick bite of bannock, then packed a satchel with two hard-boiled duck eggs, three pieces of venison jerky, and some water, and then slipped out of the cabin on tiptoe. It was quiet, peaceful. If it were a school day, Yren would be headed back up to the Longhouse for lessons with the other children. The summer meant freedom, and Yren intended to take advantage. They set out along one of the many winding dirt paths through the forest. Fat brown toads hopped out of their way as they skipped along; red squirrels and chipmunks called out warnings and dropped acorns on Yren's head.

Yren cut left through the brush and up to the clearing near Elder

Jean's trailer. On their way past they gave Story a good scratch behind his thick, furry right ear.

"Hi, Elder Jean. It's summer. No school."

"You hungry, chère?"

Yren wrinkled their nose unselfconsciously at the sight of the beans. "No, thank you. I ate."

Jean chuckled. "Off to see your friends then?" Jean never took his eyes off the simmering beans.

Yren startled, but if anyone would understand it would be Elder Jean. "Yeah. You caught me."

"You be careful out there. Or we'll come looking." Story came up from behind and wormed his massive head under Yren's arm. He stuck his cold, wet nose in Yren's left ear and licked Yren's cheek. The tether, asleep in Yren's enormous afro, shifted in its slumber, gently nudging Story's muzzle away.

"I will." Yren giggled.

"A la prochaine," Jean looked up from his cooking fire and winked, sending Yren on their way.

Yren took off running, and their tether began to vibrate with anticipation and excitement. Past Elder Jean's place there were no more well-worn paths, just wilderness. Yren hurlted over a fallen log and into the deep woods. The forest was alive with colour, motion, and sound. The hairs on the back of Yren's neck began to tingle and it seemed as though the tether were sending some sort of ultrasonic signal out into the wild. Yren and the tether's connection was like a broadcast antenna, and with it they could reach out to all the creatures of the forest and tune

in.

At first the sensation was overwhelming, a disorientating static that crackled just behind Yren's eyes. Was it another panic attack coming on? Yren closed their eyes and took a few steadying breaths. Yren took a knee and dug the fingers of their left hand deep into the loose soil of the forest floor. The signals amplified, intensified. Yren felt a bit nauseated. "Focus. You have to *focus*."

A twig snapped in the brush a few metres off. Yren startled and opened their eyes suddenly, and staring straight back was a lithe, white-tailed doe. She seemed a bit startled herself, but curious. She kept direct eye contact as she approached Yren, her dark nostrils twitching as she took in Yren's scent.

"Hello," Yren smiled. Gathering their weight beneath them, Yren stood slowly and took another set of deep breaths. The doe raised her head as well and blinked sweetly. Yren and the doe took a few moments, breathing together, synching, standing eye-to-eye. Then in one swift movement, agreeing silently in the same instant, they both took off running.

The sensation was exhilarating. The muscles in Yren's legs pulsed with inhuman strength. Their lungs expanded and contracted like bellows; their heart beat like a drum. The deer leapt through the woods with agility and grace, and Yren somehow matched her stride for stride. Together they sprang over fallen longs and through trickling streams with ease and at unimaginable speed. Yren's entire body vibrated with delight.

They paused on the banks of the gentle, tree-lined river. The sun had risen high into the cloud-streaked sky. The day had grown hot. Just as the doe lowered her lips to the cool water, so too did Yren. Looking at each other once more, the deer shuddered a nipping blackfly from her rump. The sting surprised Yren and they were both jolted out of their connection. The doe casually trotted off back into the deep brush.

Yren stood at the water's edge for a few moments, the sun beating down on them. They slipped out of their boots, tossed them over by a mossy stump, and let the cool river wash over their bare feet. Yren took a seat and flipped open their satchel for a snack. The tether twittered at the back of Yren's sweaty neck happily. A lazy breeze drifted off the water and over Yren's body and Yren caught a whiff of their own pungent stink.

Yren had reached that age when their own body never ceased to surprise them, and not always in the best ways. Yren never used to smell like this before. They had also grown several inches taller in the past month and had started sprouting hair where there had been none before. It was awkward and uncomfortable and quite often very embarrassing. Yren stood and took in their own reflection in a calm patch of water. They turned from left to right to admire their face at different angles, picking out resemblances. Yren had Aba's nose. Yren had Ama's eyes and mouth. Yren slipped off their shirt, ran their hands across their chest and sighed at their reflection in mild disappointment. Yren heard Ama's voice in their head: *Everything you are is right.* Yren held their hands out in front of them to regard their disproportionate palms. It was a strange body to Yren, not quite what they wanted, but it was a strong body. *Everything you are is right.*

Raising an elbow, Yren took another sniff of their armpit and immediately decided a swim was in order. They tossed the rest of their clothes and the satchel over by the mossy stump with the boots and then waded out into the calm river. The water was warmer than Yren expected. The rocks beneath their feet were rounded, smooth, and slick with algae; it made Yren wobble. Once the water reached waist height, Yren held their nose and plunged the rest of their body under. When they surfaced, Yren let out a whoop that echoed off the trees before settling into a floating position on their back. By keeping their lungs full of air they could drift along with little effort.

Yren's tether was as much at home in the water as Yren. It relaxed its grip and slid along the length of Yren's body, then drifted off dancing in the gentle current. Yren let the water carry them further into the middle of the river. Here the bottom was murky, deeper. Something underneath the water tapped Yren on the backside. Yren let out a surprised shriek, dropped their feet below, and steadied themselves in the water. "What was that?!"

A broad furry face with shining black eyes broke the surface of the water a few metres to Yren's left. Sneezing cheerfully, then brushing out its thick whiskers, the river otter rolled over and exposed his bloated belly to the sun. A second otter paddled up on its back beside the first, combing out the fur on its tummy with its massive webbed paws.

Yren took a mouthful of water and sent a graceful stream arching through the air and onto the belly of the closest otter. "You scared me!" Yren chuckled and then plunged beneath the water. Yren felt their tether latch on to the nape of their neck as they dove. The tether sent several feathery tendrils down the length of Yren's spine. A familiar tingling sensation washed over Yren. When they opened their eyes under water, Yren found themself swimming steadily below the surface, the otters spiralling around them in dizzy circles.

Yren touched the bottom. The riverbed was strewn with smooth, round stones of every imaginable shape and size. Yren dug their fingers into the riverbed and pulled themself along the bottom. Their new otter playmates swam along either side. Yren could see! The river bottom had been a cloud of murky water before, yet now Yren could see. They could smell the fish swimming just slightly upstream. It took no effort at all to hold their breath

for five minutes at a time. The three friends would swim to the surface and glide along on their backs, warming themselves in the summer sun, and then dive back down to the depths of the riverbed to dance and play in the gentle current over and over again.

Yren came to the surface for a breath after their last dive and noticed something odd along the shoreline. There was movement over by the mossy stump where Yren had dumped their things. "Oh, no ..." They glanced quickly over one shoulder and saw their otter buddies bobbing on the river's surface. "I'm sorry. I have to go!" Yren paddled for the shore. They could feel the connection fading the further away they swam, and within a few moments it was gone entirely.

Where the water grew shallow enough Yren stood up to walk. An enormous, furry grey bum wiggled in the open mouth of Yren's satchel. "I should have known! Shoo! Shoo!" The masked face of a chubby racoon glared back at Yren incredulously. Yren struggled to gain their footing on the slippery rocks, waving their arms widely in an effort to scare away the ring-tailed thief. "Shoo!"

Yren watched the racoon snatch up the satchel and dart into the woods.

"UGH! Are you kidding me?"

They dressed hastily, first throwing their shirt over themselves and then one boot. Yren hopped along a few steps, torn between keeping up the chase and getting the second boot on properly. Yren sat down on the rocky shore, squished a wet foot into the warm, tanned hide of their slouchy boot, then leapt back up to their feet. They had temporarily lost sight of the racoon but yelled out in the general direction. "Come back here!"

Yren sprinted into the woods, listening with all their senses for any signs of the racoon. "This way," Yren whispered to themself and darted through the brush. Yren wasn't the best tracker, but Nyx Quay had certainly shown them a few things. Here and there they picked up the certain trail of the absconding furry fiend: a morsel of half-chewed jerky; a five-fingered paw print in the slightly damp earth; the broken twigs from a bit of brush; drag marks made by the satchel. Yren followed the reckless path made by the racoon all the way to the edge of a sun-dappled clearing covered with wild strawberry plants.

"Gotcha!" Yren caught sight of the chubby bum of the racoon several metres away in the middle of the field and took off running in that direction. It appeared he had stopped to pluck a few berries for himself and had forgotten he was ever being chased. The racoon grabbed up the satchel once more, scampering for the trees on the other side of the field. Being quite a bit smaller than Yren and dragging the heavy sack behind him, the racoon was surely outmatched. Yren was sprinting at top speed, their eyes locked on the bottle brush tail of the little thief in front of them, when they tripped and lost their footing. Yren came crashing down hard, knocking the wind out of themself.

It took a few moments for Yren to catch their breath. They rolled over to their back and lay in the middle of the field, covered in smashed berries and furious. Yren sat up slowly and looked around. No sign of the racoon at all. Yren swore under their breath in frustration. What had they even tripped over?

Yren extended a hand past their feet and touched the smooth metal surface of the ... gun? They had seen hunting rifles, but this was something else. It was thicker than a rifle, an oblong hunk of metal painted bright yellow with stripes of black and white across the length of it. Yren dragged it over to inspect it closer. It was heavy, smooth. There was a numbered dial on the stock that appeared to be broken, and a cloth strap attached to its body so that it could be carried more easily. Yren felt their

breath quickening. This wasn't an ordinary rifle or gun. This was something else. Yren scanned the immediate area with their eyes and crouched down low. What if whoever had lost this ... thing ... was still here?

Yren could feel the panic coming. They could feel the blood rushing to their ears, hear their own heart pounding in their chest, and their vision went a little blurry. Yren dug their fingers into the soft ground and took several deep breaths. The tether cooed and pulsed in an attempt to soothe.

They were staring blankly at the ground when their vision came back into focus. Something silvery and shiny caught the afternoon light. Yren recognized the shape immediately. Yren's fingers tickled the length of the silver chain down to the delicate little hamsa charm attached to it. The hamsa was a little hand-shaped ornament, with a single open eye at its centre. Yren's mother wore a charm just like ...

"Ama?"

Yren suddenly felt like the wind had been knocked out of them again. This was Ama's necklace, Yren was almost sure of it. More than that, the clasp was still intact and the chain had not been broken. Yren turned the charm over and over in one hand and held the gun firmly with the other. A sharp, snapping sound echoed across the clearing from the tree line to the west. A broken twig? An approaching animal? Perhaps something ... or someone come to claim that which they'd left behind. Yren didn't wish to wait to find out. Making use of the strap, they slung the heavy metal object over one shoulder and aimed their body in the direction of home.

"All bodies
are good bodies."

- Charlotte Barkla

CHAPTER SEVEN

Yren had no control over their dreams but had developed a bit of sway over their own waking thoughts. Whenever a flash of memory from the day of the accident overtook their mind's eye, Yren always made a conscious effort not to stay there. They didn't like to dwell on the events of that day. Trudging back through the familiar woods and towards the Village with Ama's necklace wrapped around their hand unleashed a flood of unwelcome recollections.

Don't be afraid. We're here to protect you if anything goes wrong. We're safe, way out here. No one is going to get hurt, baby, we promise. Just concentrate on what you're doing.

Yren flinched the memories away, changed focus. They tucked the hamsa necklace in a small pocket and took the rifle down off their shoulders. Unfamiliar tech. Yren had never seen anything like it before. Maybe it was a relic of the Old World? Maybe it had been through some great, distant uprising? Wouldn't that be exciting? Surely the weapon had some story to tell. Maybe Nyx or one of the other hunters could even get it to work again! If it worked, maybe it could be useful. If it turned out to be useful, maybe Yren wouldn't get in too much trouble. It would have been foolish to leave the thing behind, mouldering in the mossy woods.

When Yren arrived on the edges of town it was growing close to dusk. Swarms of gnats swirled in the peach-coloured sky so thickly that Yren sometimes had to shut their eyes and mouth up tight to pass through. The burden of the gun was heavy, and their shoulders ached from the weight. They crept past Elder Jean's place stealthily, keeping off the main paths and sticking to the taller scrub. Best to remain unseen for now they thought. Though the walk had been long they still had no solid plan for what to do next. The last thing Yren wanted was to be gripped up by Elder Jean with a rifle or whatever this was slung across their back. Crouched down in the bushes, Yren could see lamp light shimmering in the windows of the trailer, but no sign of Jean, or Story for that matter.

"This is stupid," Yren whispered to themselves. "Move. Move before you get caught." Yren scampered past the trailer as quietly as they could manage, careful to dodge the clockers as they went along.

The Village was not without its defenses. Motion detectors and other such devices, now commonly called clockers, had been set up long ago as an early warning device. It had been improved bit by bit, age after age since its creation by the first settlers. But no stranger had entered these woods in years, and certainly not in Yren's lifetime. At least not that they were aware. Even still, the perimeter was maintained as a precaution, repaired regularly by the elders. Information from the clockers was steadily fed to a terminal in the Longhouse, where someone routinely checked on the incoming data. Guard duty was done in rotations. It was a boring, thankless task. Sometimes Augi would keep Unti Alton company when it was their turn.

There had been a time when run-ins with outsiders were more anticipated, sometimes even welcomed. Yren had heard the stories when Ama and Aba and Unti spoke of their own childhoods. Stories of visits to other settlements. Hard to believe in it now, the existence of other villages, other people, other lives. There had been a trade network, and a centralized school for advanced learning among other things. There had also been raids. Roving bands of violent, aggressive hunters went looking for easy targets.

The Village had endured by being both remote and primarily self-sufficient. Of course sometimes folks journeyed out, based on some pre-arranged accord with a neighbouring settlement

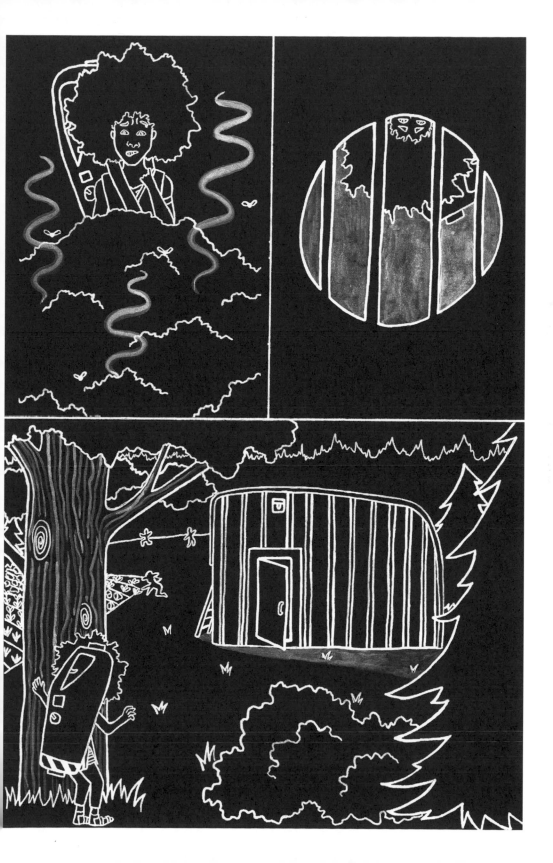

over the comms. Sometimes those folks returned with new tech, new information, new partners, or even new families. Though by the time Ama and Aba were teenagers even that practice had grown rare. The people of the Village had grown increasingly cautious as more and more often when folks left, for one reason or another, they did not return.

Then came the Plague. Word first arrived over the comms from the more populated settlements in the south. A virulent influenza had emerged, more aggressive than the ones seen in previous years. It was thought that the virus was a mutated strain, something against which folks had yet to adapt. Bulletins announced the flu had claimed the lives of hundreds within a matter of days, and thousands in the weeks to come. People fled the crowded cities for more remote towns in an effort to put distance between themselves and the Plague, but they carried the disease with them, infected others. All attempts to contain the damage proved futile. It took a little time, but eventually the Plague arrived for the People of the Village.

But for the People of the Village, there had also come the tethers. The little hovering healers had managed a miraculous last-minute rescue. Sadly, it seemed rather localized. None of the other settlements the Village remained in contact with had confirmed reports of any such creatures. Chatter over the comms dwindled over the months that followed, then disappeared altogether. Six years went by with nothing more than static over the comms. For better or for worse it seemed that there may not be much of an "out there" either to barter or to reckon with. Hunting parties went out from time to time, returning victorious, but always having seen no other signs of ongoing human life. There had been a time of collective mourning from most of the adults and then acceptance, even relief. The land and the water here were good. While the desert consumed what lay beyond, in this place nature had continued to spring up in glorious abundance. The people of the Village were healthy and happy and, for the most part, unafraid. Though someone always maintained the watch, guard duty these days was more like keeping the lamp lit.

Still, Yren was in no hurry to announce their return. What Yren really needed was time to think more clearly. If only there were some place to hide the weapon until they knew what to do.

Yren's bladder ached. Several metres ahead there were a set of composting latrines, surrounded by a small processing station that gradually converted the waste material into soil. Every few months the soil would be collected and then dispersed as fertilizer. Towering mounds of nutrient rich fertilizer stood piled high against the south wall of the processing station. The smell was sharp, earthy; not particularly pleasant, but tolerable. There was no one around. Latrines weren't the sort of place where people lingered unnecessarily after all. Yren considered tossing the rifle into one of the mounds. No one would go looking for it there. Then again, it would certainly be discovered if anyone came to scatter the fertilizer. Besides, what if Yren wanted to retrieve the thing later themself? They would have to go digging through the deepening pile of ... No, Yren thought better of it.

Yren emptied their bladder then exited the latrine and walked uphill a bit to wash their hands in the basin fed by the gigantic nearby cistern. The cistern was a series of massive sunken vessels used to collect rainwater run-off. Yren knelt on the ground and gazed down the mouth of one of the drains. What if Yren dropped the rifle down into the tank? A bit of rope, perhaps. They could secure one end to the rifle, lower it deep enough to be hidden but suspended above the water in the tank, and then tie the other end off to the bars of the mouth of the drain. It wasn't a perfect plan, but it was better than nothing. As long as no one noticed or took any special interest in the visible knot. Surely no one would trouble themselves to look down a storm drain. Right?

Rope. There would be rope in the supply shed.

Yren swiftly but quietly made their way toward the supply shed set back in the woods a short distance away from their family cabin. Occasionally they ducked behind a tree or some bit of scrub to avoid detection. Yren dropped down and lay in the dirt next to a fallen and uncharacteristically thick old birch tree. A wave of embarrassment swept over them. "This is silly," Yren chuckled to themselves and then came out of hiding. There was no one else in sight. Yren took a few deep breaths and convinced their body to casually walk up to the shed, though they could still hear their heart beating in their ears. The door was unlatched. Yren had one hand on the handle to the shed door, but their eyes on the woods around the cabin, when the door suddenly burst open.

"What the—" Yren startled, stumbled backwards, lost their footing, and landed hard on their backside.

Augi's flushed face appeared in the darkened doorway. "What are you doing?"

"Augi! You scared the life out of me!"

Augi emerged from the shed and gently shut the door behind him. "What are you doing? What is that?" Augi's gaze landed squarely on the rifle.

"Nothing. Nothing!" Yren scrambled to their feet. Augi excitedly advanced on their sibling to get a closer look.

"Where did you find ... that?"

"Will you keep your voice down?"

"Why? Where've you been all day?" Augi made a grab for the

rifle.

"That's none of your business!" Yren shrieked back, and slapped Augi's hand away.

"Lemme hold it, Yren. I wanna see!"

In their squabbling neither of the siblings heard the approaching footsteps until it was too late.

Unti glared at Yren and Augi somberly. "Bring. It. Here."

CHAPTER EIGHT

Yren sheepishly walked over to Unti and surrendered the rifle. Without another word, Unti Alton rounded on his heels and into the cabin. Augi and Yren did not need to be told to follow.

"Unti Alton ... what is it?" Yren, Augi, and Unti stood in the common room of the cabin. A gentle breeze pushed through the open shutters. Flies danced here and there over the solid timbre walls.

"A tool." Unti calmly held the heavy metal object and turned it slowly around in his hands, regarding it carefully. "Perhaps, a weapon." Unti's gaze landed on Yren and Augi with a little suspicion and more than a little concern. He was silent for a moment and then said very sternly, "Certainly not a toy."

Augi and Yren immediately looked down at the wooden slats of the floor.

"Where did you get this?"

Yren never took their eyes off the floor as they answered. "Strawberries. I went looking for strawberries. There's a field –"

"—Almost ten kilometers away, yes, I know it. That's a long walk for you two."

Yren looked up cautiously.

"Yren went without me! I wasn't there!"

"Augi wasn't there, Unti."

"Then it was a long and *potentially dangerous* walk."

Yren stared at the floor some more.

"But what does it *do*, Unti?" Augi could scarcely contain himself.

Unti pursed his lips and hoisted the tool higher in his arms to look at it more closely. "I'm not entirely sure, my love. Whatever it did, it now appears to be broken."

"I bet Aba would know," Yren whispered.

"Yes. Your father was a brilliant Maker. But so am I."

"Unti, you're an artist. Aba was an engineer."

"Engineers and artists aren't all that different ... depending on who you talk to."

Augi and Yren chuckled quietly, and when Unti laughed a little in return Yren and Augi both breathed a sigh of relief. Perhaps they weren't in as much trouble as they had thought.

"Well there's only one thing for it," said Unti resolutely. Yren and Augi shot nervous glances at one another. "This has to be taken to the Village Council." Unti made a few adjustments to the supper waiting on the low table for his family, gathered up a small pack of something to eat for himself, and slung the rifle over one shoulder. "Wash yourselves and eat. Clear the table and tidy up when you're done. It won't be very long before I get back." Unti made to leave but then stopped in the doorway with his back to Yren and Augi. "I expect you both to be here when I do."

When Unti was out of sight both sibs exhaled audibly.

Augi rounded on his sibling. "What have you done?"

Yren's face crumpled in consternation. "There's something they're not telling us, Augi. I can feel it." Yren slumped down on a cushion beside the table and pushed a few bits of food around absentmindedly with a dirty finger.

"Well, come on then," Augi prodded.

"What?"

Augi shook his head and rolled his eyes. "We're going to that Council meeting."

CHAPTER NINE

Yren and Augi sprinted through the woods unnoticed to the Longhouse.

"This way," Augi whispered, and then stealthily shimmied up a drainpipe, using a few ridges in the shipping container for leverage. Yren stood there, mouth agape, and then swiftly followed Augi's lead.

Once they'd reach the top, Yren whispered, "How in the world did you know to—"

Augi flapped his arms wildly in Yren's face then put a finger to his own lips. Yren got the message immediately. Augi slithered on his belly past the stored feed and toward a small opening in the floor. Yren followed suit. Out of sight, from the shelter of the second story of the Longhouse, Augi and Yren could listen in on the elders of the Village Council. Among those gathered Yren could make out both Nyx and Stokely Quay, Elder Jean and his constant companion Story, and the eldest members of each of the fifteen families, which included their Unti, Alton Stone. There was a perceptible shift in the room as the polite chatter of greetings morphed into curiosity and concern.

Stokely raised an arm and silence fell. Her tone was measured, even. "Alton! What's all of this about? Why have you summoned us?"

"Council members, I present..." Unti took the rifle down from his shoulders by the strap and laid it plainly on the floor in the middle of the circle for all to see. Some of the Council members shifted, stood to get a better view.

"How did you come by this, Alton?" Nyx was calm, but there was an edge to her voice. Yren and Augi immediately picked up

on what her voice tried to hide: fear.

"About ten clicks from camp, due east. In a meadow." Alton shot a quick glance at Elder Jean. It wasn't quite long enough for anyone to notice except for Yren. "It's broken."

"Well at least he's kept your name out of it," Augi whispered.

"So far," Yren replied.

Nyx came forward and took the tool in her weathered hands. She looked it over carefully. "It's not a weapon," she declared. An audible sigh of relief shot through the room. Nyx held the erstwhile rifle in attack position and took aim with it, squinting one eye down the length of it to its firing end. She made certain not to point it at any one in the circle, but rather at the far wall instead. "There's no scope, and no reasonable place to attach one." She lowered the firing end. "And it's heavy. Too heavy for combat. This wasn't made for fighting."

Nyx sauntered over to Elder Jean Lemieux and held the tech out to him. Jean took it, reluctantly. "What say you, old man?"

Yren watched carefully as Elder Jean and Unti Alton exchanged another subtle glance.

Jean rested the tech in his lap and took a long look around the room, then cleared his throat before he spoke. "It's missing a power source. Zero point maybe? No, Crystalline. Proximity activated."

"Was there a recognizable power source where you found it, Alton?" Stokely urged him on.

"I... didn't find it."

Jean was quiet for another few moments then cocked his head in Unti Alton's direction. "Yren?"

There was mild confusion among the members of the Council. All assembled traded questioning glances.

Alton spoke up. "Yep. I asked you to keep an eye on them."

"They're growing up Alton. You can't shelter them from everything. I'd have known if something went wrong; I'd have felt it. Story would've –"

Unti balled his fists up, choked back a bitter tear. "The same way you didn't know when something happened to my brother? And your niece?"

Nyx came forward and stood between the two of them. "Now, Alton—wait a minute. There's no way anyone could have predicted that accident. You know that."

Elder Jean stood up slowly. "Not a day goes by where I don't wish we'd found Dayle and Aduke. Nothing puts a hole in your heart quite like an empty grave. Your brother deserved better than that. And so did my sweet niece. I know we've... had our differences in the past, but believe me when I say I love those children, Alton. They're my flesh and blood. I won't let nothin' happen to 'em. But Yren has to explore the boundaries of their abilities. We've discussed this. That child is gifted. That child is a gift to all of us. I've seen a lot in my time on this Earth and a free, Black-Indigenous child like that... is a blessing. I won't tamper with it. I won't cage it. Do you understand me? They need to be free."

"But what if it isn't safe, Jean?" Unti Alton's voice was raised, sharp. "Sure, we haven't seen anybody out there in *years*, but maybe we've all gotten a little too comfortable. That tech—"

"... is a fracking cannon. Used for ore extraction. Mining. It's a glorified water pistol. Nothing more."

"But—"

"And that child is safer than any of you could possibly imagine."

Unti glared hot and hard at Elder Jean Lemieux. Stokely Quay broke the silence. "We'll double the watch for a few moons, Alton." Stokely came forward and placed a hand on Nyx's shoulder, who still stood ready between Unti and Elder Jean. "And maybe Nyx and the hunters can do a few extra sweeps." Nyx glanced down at Stokely, lovingly. "Just to be sure."

"Absolutely," Nyx returned her loving partner's warm look. She then sternly turned her gaze back to Unti. "We'll take care of it, Alton."

Unti seemed ready to pounce on Elder Jean at any moment. His focus was locked on the old man. Story got up from his place of rest and nuzzled his face into Elder Jean's open palm, then shot a low rumbling growl and mean look up at Unti Alton.

"Alton!" Nyx tried again. Unti took his eyes off Jean and looked at her. Nyx took Alton's face in both her hands warmly. "We won't let you lose another."

Yren watched as something in Alton broke. A single tear rolled down his cheek and into Nyx's hand.

Augi pinched Yren's elbow gently. "Let's go," he whispered. The siblings scurried down the side of the Longhouse the same way they'd come in and ran full speed back toward the cabin. They emptied the table of supper, now gone cold, scraping the platters into a compost pail and rinsing the dishes in the basin as quickly as they could manage without breaking anything. They worked together swiftly, wordlessly. There would be time to discuss what they had overheard later.

When Unti arrived a few short moments later, Yren and Augi expected to receive another barrage of sharp words and stern warnings. Instead, Unti Alton went straight to his room and shut the door, barely glancing at either Yren or Augi.

CHAPTER TEN

Grief is like a shadow; it follows. It looms in the corners of the bright room of your world so that whenever you turn your head to face it, there it is on the edges. Even when the sun is at its highest, even when the light is at its brightest, the shadow remains. Maybe it is even because the light of life is so vibrant, so rich and so warm, that the shadow of grief seems all the darker.

Unti tried to work the grief away. Unti was a Maker after all, a potter. Spending hour after hour in his studio throwing clay – producing gorgeous plates, vases, and vessels – Unti tried to shape the earth into something useful. He tried to make something beautiful out of the feelings he hid from his niblings, Augi and Yren. It made Unti distant, though that was the last thing that he wanted to be. It just didn't seem proper to be that deeply saddened in the face of these also-grieving children. He wanted to smile bravely and to lavish the love he could no longer give to his brother on his brother's children. More than just feeding and sheltering them, he wanted to nurture, inspire, and protect them. Unti wanted to be strong, to be hopeful. Yet somehow the darkness loomed.

When Augi first arrived into this world he was spoiled with love. Then Yren had gotten sick, and while it wasn't necessarily their intention, the bulk of his parents' time and attention went to Yren. Augi often ached for any kind of notice and affection. It made him rambunctious, a bit mischievous. He did everything he could think of to elicit laughter from the people around him, but especially from his parents. Since the loss of their parents Augi needed to feel loved even more desperately. He was so used to being a joyful child, or rather so used to being loved for being joyful, that he was afraid to be any other way lest people stop loving him. So Augi kept smiling. Even through his grief, Augi made it his business to make others laugh. He leaned in to being joyful in an effort to skip over his own pain. If he could just keep people happy everything might be okay. But three months had passed since the accident, and people-pleasing had begun to wear on him. He resented the effort to keep smiling. Yren had noticed how Augi had grown increasingly secretive. Yren had noticed that they weren't the only one of the two sibs who disappeared for long stretches of time.

Yren never wanted to press Augi too hard about how he felt or what he was up to because they didn't need the pressure of having to answer those questions themself. Escaping the Village to explore their budding abilities was Yren's only comfort lately. While there were several people in the Village who had developed heightened skills once they had been healed by their tethers, Yren's gifts seemed to extend beyond the unusual and right to the extraordinary. It had been instilled in Yren for years by their parents that it was best to keep certain things private. People often feared what they could not understand. Sometimes Ama and Aba would take Yren out to some secluded corner of the wilds to practice, away from prying eyes. That's why they were out in the Barrens on the day of the accident. Practice.

Yren had dreamt about that day countless times. The sequence of events had played out over and over again in their mind's eye. In the dark of night it seemed the shadow of grief touched everything in sight, so that Yren had no choice but to be consumed by it. Yren would often wake up startled, drenched in sweat, their eyes streaming tears. Sometimes Yren would lie there in the dark and just let themself cry, listening to the sounds of Augi's ragged breathing from his bed across the room. Sometimes, when the shadows were too much to bear, Yren would slip out of bed past their sleeping sibling, past the common room and the door to Unti's room, out the main door of the cabin and into the night.

There was a small outcrop of boulders nestled by the water's edge just outside their family's cabin. Atop one of these massive boulders there was a humble pile of stones about a metre high, stacked there by Yren's ancestors to make a fire pit. Yren would make a small fire to keep the dark at bay and sit there for hours tending the fire. On clear nights the sky was lit up by a billion stars. When Ama was alive she would point them out, she would name them, she would tell their stories to her children. Sitting there Yren tried to remember the names of those stars, tried to remember the stories behind the names. It brought Ama back, just a little. So on a hot summer night, when Yren awoke sweating and panicked from yet another nightmare, they already knew what to do.

Augi snored gently from across the room. Yren could just make out his arm dangling off the edge of his bed. Yren carefully slipped out of bed and crept through the cabin in their nightshirt and bare feet to the hearth in the common room. The stone facade of the fireplace was cold to the touch. Yren quietly opened the small metal tin on the mantel and removed the igniter. They took down their satchel from a hook by the front door and slung it over one shoulder. Yren stood there by the door for a few moments, listening for any signs that Unti may be awake. Hearing nothing, Yren unlatched the door, softly pulling it open so its metal hinges wouldn't squeak, and then slipped out into the night.

Yren shuffled quietly across the deck and down the wooden stairs. A summer wind blew gently through the trees. The ground was cool, damp, and littered with a fine layer of pine needles. Yren walked on the balls of their feet and carefully made their way in darkness to the lean-to next to the supply shed. They grabbed an empty two-gallon bucket from the shed and selected a single, pre-cut log from the wood pile in the lean-to. Yren balanced the log on their right shoulder and held it steady with their right hand and carried the empty pail in their left.

The weight was a strain on their shoulders and the darkness was a strain on their eyes. Yren feared that one misstep on a slippery rock would cause a serious fall. They took small, cautious steps in the direction of the water, making sure each foot was firmly placed. Their neck ached from the effort, and then began to tingle warmly. Yren slowly became aware of a softly pulsing glow just behind their left ear; it illuminated the path before them. They didn't have to turn around to know. "You're late," Yren whispered to the tether. "Thanks for the help." Together they reached the smooth expanse of boulders where Yren could set down their burden and get to work.

It was Aba that had taught Yren how to safely build a fire. First, Yren filled the metal pail with water from the lake. They held the heavy pail with both hands, the bucket dangling between their legs, and waddled awkwardly from the water's edge back to the fire pit. This way when it came time to put the fire out, or if the fire suddenly grew out of control it could easily be doused. Next Yren gathered up a bundle of the thin, dead branches scattered here and there. Then they plucked up a small heap of brittle pine needles and dried out pine cones by holding out the bottom edges of their nightshirt and using it like a makeshift basket. When they had enough kindling, Yren arranged the various components in the fire pit strategically so the things that burned fastest would be at the base. Then Yren struck the igniter and let a bit of blue-hot flame set the kindling ablaze. It took patience, skill, and a bit of coaxing but Yren had a decent fire going shortly.

Yren sat down and let the warmth and light of the fire wash over them, silently watching the flames dance. The fire was bright, dynamic. It transformed itself, shifting colour and changing shape with every breath it took. They set their gaze on its centre, the white-hot heart of the fire itself, and found their mind pulled deeper into the alluring glow. Under Yren's

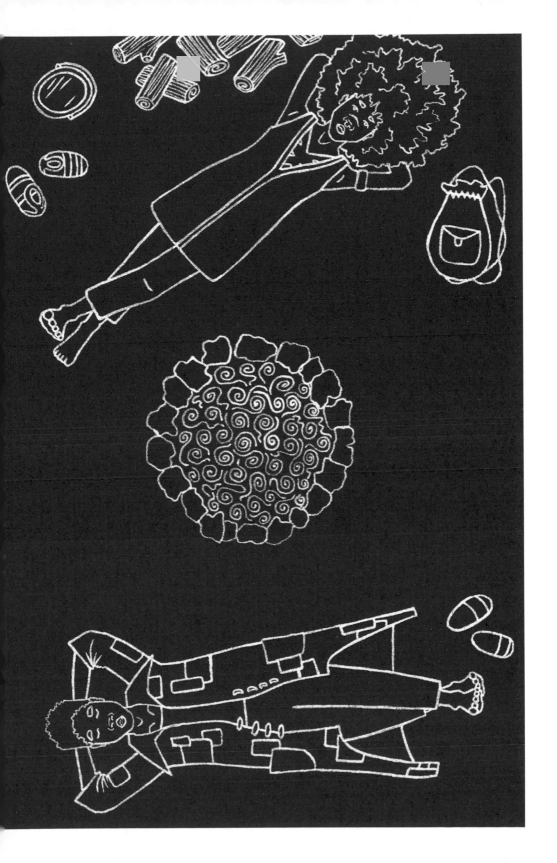

watchful eye, the flames took on irregular forms, shapes that did not at first seem probable. *Just concentrate on what you're doing.* The fire condensed into a perfect sphere; then collapsed again into a four-sided triangle; then morphed once more until it solidified into a cube slowly rotating on its axis. Suddenly the log popped, split, and shifted loudly in the fire pit, breaking Yren's focus. The flames returned to normal.

"Hey, fire bug." Augi called out from a short distance, then emerged from the darkness. Had he seen?

"You scared me."

"Sorry." Augi plopped down on the boulder next to Yren and smiled sleepily. "Another dream?"

Yren's tether drifted through the air in the space between them, still glowing slightly in the dark. Yren could tell from Augi's expression that he'd witnessed nothing. Relieved, they nodded guiltily, then quickly turned their gaze back toward the fire. Yren picked a bit of dirt from underneath their fingernails as they spoke. "I see them falling... almost every night. They fall and I can't help them all over again." The siblings sat there in the fire light, in silence for a few moments, the shadow of grief looming all around them.

"I'll go get another log," said Augi, finally. Yren took a few deep breaths to steady themselves while Augi went up to the lean-to and then came back with his arms full of firewood. Augi placed a log on the fire and then lay back with his arms behind his head, staring up at the night sky. Yren smiled and did the same.

"So many stars. It makes me feel so small sometimes," Yren marvelled. "You could just... float away and into forever; there's so much out there *out there*. Ya know?"

"Yeah. Maybe they're up there watching right now," Augi cooed. The space between Yren's brows wrinkled as they shot a questioning look at Augi.

"Ama and Aba, I mean."

"Oh. Maybe." Yren smiled wistfully, then sighed. "All our ancestors, known and unknown. Everyone we've ever loved who's left this world and gone on to the next. Right? All the answers to all the questions. *The Loving Spirit of the Universe*." Yren's voice broke. Without looking or pulling it into plain view, they slipped a hand inside their satchel and delicately traced the lines of Ama's necklace. "Wouldn't that be wild?"

"Yren?"

"M-hm?"

"Did you know all that stuff about Elder Jean? About him being Ama's uncle, I mean?"

"Ama never talked about her mother much, but she said a few things... about how her mother's side of the family wasn't particularly pleased about her mother marrying a ... nevermind. I didn't know for sure, but I'd sort of guessed. Doesn't matter now anyway. We're here; they aren't." Yren searched Augi's expression in the dim light but couldn't quite discern their sibling's thoughts. "You sneak up there a lot? To listen to Council meetings? You climbed up there like you'd done it once or twice before..."

"I don't sneak. I just pay attention." Augi looked Yren squarely in the eyes. "People around here have all sorts of secrets." Yren felt their cheeks go hot. Augi turned his gaze back to considering the stars. "Everyone we've ever loved and lost... up there with the stars. Instead of down here with us. I wish we'd gotten to say goodbye, ya know?"

"Yeah. Me too."

Augi sat up suddenly and got to his feet, wiping the dirt from his backside. "I'm going back to bed. You coming?"

"You go ahead. I'll be in, in a bit."

"Love you."

"I love you too, Bubs."

Yren watched as Augi's silhouette faded into the night. They watched the fire die down as the birds began singing in the distance. Eventually, they picked up the pail and doused the remaining embers in the fire pit and headed back toward the cabin. Yren thought about the day ahead. Unti would be awake soon. They'd all have breakfast and then separately set out to salvage something meaningful from their daylit hours. But the night would come again, and they would still be three lonely people, living under the same roof, living under the same shadow of grief.

Yren couldn't bear the thought of telling their family the accident was all their fault.

CHAPTER ELEVEN

The sun was strong, bright, and high in the sky. The birds chased one another from tree to tree, singing. In much the same way, the small children of the Village mimicked the behaviour of the birds – playing tag excitedly, screaming loudly, laughing gleefully. It was a gorgeous summer day. Everyone seemed to be in high spirits; everyone except for Yren. Perhaps a walk would help? Yren allowed their mind to wander, and their feet to follow suit. Yren walked about aimlessly, and eventually found themselves just outside the Orchard.

Yren had avoided coming here for months, but left to their own devices it was where their feet had led them nonetheless. They took a deep, stabilizing breath and walked slowly into the shadowed rows of trees. Yren slipped off their shoes and dragged their feet in the cool earth of the paths between the neatly planted trees. It was almost meditative. They watched the dappled light streaming through the leaves dance across the dark skin of their bare arms. The smell was glorious. The scent of fresh fruit permeated the air – apricots, peaches, and plums. Yren couldn't help but smile. It was a marvelous place, full of life.

In the centre of the Orchard was a small circular clearing lined with wooden benches. This clearing made a separation between the Living Orchard, where folks gathered and tended to the abundance the land had to offer, and the Orchard of the Dead. Yren took a seat and stared off into the grove of trees on the other side of the clearing. They were so lost in thought that they didn't hear the approaching footsteps.

"Hello, Yren." Stokely beamed. Something about the way the light hit her back made her look almost angelic.

"Hello, Elder Quay."

Stokely chuckled. "You can just call me Stokely, Yren." She came around the back of the bench and sat down next to Yren. "And what brings you to the Orchard today, my dear?"

Yren shrugged, then unexpectedly found tears welling up in their eyes.

"Oh, honey. Come here." Stokely held her arms out wide and before Yren knew what they were doing found that they had thrown themself into Stokely's embrace. The two of them stayed that way for a few moments in silence. In the distance behind the two of them Yren could make out children running between the trees, people gathering small harvests to take home. Yren was slightly embarrassed, but it seemed no one was paying much attention to either of them. Yren pulled away slowly from Stokely, wiping the tears from their face.

"Would you like to learn some more about your people; where your ancestors come from?" Stokely asked, gently.

Yren flinched, nodded.

Stokely stood up from the bench and extended a hand. Yren took it, and together they walked into the Orchard of the Dead.

"Well, now... where to start. Has anyone ever told you about Ifedayo?"

Yren shook their head silently. They were still a bit too choked up to speak. Stokely pointed out a single, graceful tree. Etched on a small plaque staked into the ground in front of this tree was a name, *Ifedayo Dwyer*, and two dates, *2028 - 2092*.

"This is your Great Grandparent, and one of the founders of the Village, Ifedayo. Ifedayo Dwyer arrived in Canada from Jamaica in 2049, just a few years before the peak of the Fall. She left her home to transition, to become someone new. She chose her new name from the old Yoruba. *Ifedayo*, which means *love has become joy*. It was her love for herself and the woman she was becoming that led her to this place. It was her love for her people, her determination, her intelligence, and fighting spirit that made this place a reality."

Stokely carefully guided Yren to another tree nearby. "In a place called *Tkaronto*, Ife met and fell in love with August Stone, whose family first settled here in the 1880s from across the sea in England and Germany."

"August? You mean, like Augi?"

Stokely nodded knowingly. "Though they were from very different places, August and Ifedayo understood one another in ways the rest of the world could not."

"Now, the Stone family had long ago purchased a small plot of land in Northern Ontario and built a summer home there. At the time it was land owned by the Crown, who had in fact stolen that land from the Indigenous people of Ontario. August and Ife escaped up to this tiny scrap of Algonquin whenever city life grew too much for them, which was often – whenever the world just wouldn't allow their trans, queer, brown bodies to just be." Stokely took a deep, solemn breath. "And then came the Fall."

"August and Ifedayo invited a few friends along to ride out this new chaos on their small homestead; waiting for things in the wider world to shift back to the chaos they were used to. But that never happened. More friends joined. They formed a tenuous relationship with some of the locals, a handful of the more trustworthy strangers. This collective gradually became the original Fifteen Families of The Village," Stokely smiled. "Now, Ife and August had a son, Ola, who met and married the radiant Safia. Safia had a tremendous talent for music. And Ola was a brilliant strategist and organizer. They had two children, Alton and Aduke, whom I believe you call Unti and Aba." Stokely smiled broadly. "Alton very much takes after Safia; and I see equal parts of both of your grandparents in your father. It's such a shame you never got to meet them. I know they would have adored you."

Yren winced a little. "I could never get my folks to talk very much about their parents."

"There is a peculiar thread of loss in your family line, on all sides. I imagine it was difficult for them to discuss. Ola passed suddenly – a heart attack – and then Safia shortly after. Aduke had already married your mother. You came along just a few years later. Your Aba and Unti were both grown by then, but the grief of losing both parents so quickly –" At these words, Stokely caught herself. "Well, I don't have to tell you what that must have felt like."

Yren nodded, solemnly.

Stokely continued, cautiously. "I believe that Death is merely a transition from this world to one beyond our comprehension. We are energy, all of us. And energy –"

"Can neither be created, nor destroyed." Yren completed.

"Yes. Of course, you've learned that in your studies. And so it is." Stokely wrapped a single arm around Yren and gave a gentle squeeze. "That energy continues. It goes on. Like the Orchard."

Yren gazed up at Stokely. "The Orchard?"

"Yes. At the height of the Fall, in 2053, Ifedayo thought it wise to start an orchard. She had long been a lover of plants, a collector of seeds. After Ifedayo passed away, in accordance with her wishes, she was buried here in a special section of the Orchard. So that her soul could graft to the trees. So that her essence could return to Earth, to travel endlessly toward the Loving Spirit of the Universe. From that day forward every member of the Fifteen Families that has passed on has been processed and laid to rest here, so that they may continue to nourish the land and the People in death as they had in life."

Yren's gaze darted over to a noticeable gap in the grove, a dead space that called out to be acknowledged. "You mean *almost* everyone who's died." Yren wandered over to the empty plot where the trees bearing their parents' names ought to have been.

Stokely's brown, round face shifted visibly with concern. "That must be very hard for you, not to be able to visit them properly. We tried, the elders I mean, we tried to speak to Alton about that, but without the remains Alton wouldn't allow..."

"I know."

Yren's thoughts drifted over to their grieving Unti Alton, and to the argument they'd witnessed between Unti and Elder Jean.

"Elder Quay?"

"Yes, dear?"

"Can you tell me more about how I'm related to Elder Jean?"

Stokely sighed, a bit relieved and a bit resigned. She took her arm from around Yren and folded both her hands carefully in her own lap. "That would be through your mother's branch of

the family tree." Stokely extended her hand and once Yren took it, led Yren away to yet another grouping of trees in the Orchard of the Dead.

"This is the tree of your ancestor, Irène Jakot." Yren immediately heard the likeness in pronunciation to their own name. They gazed up at Stokely's gently smiling face, the warm light haloed around her head. Stokely truly seemed to be an all-knowing angel. How many more stories were behind this loving woman's eyes?

"Irène belonged to the Huron-Wendat, the Indigenous caretakers of this land. She was a remarkable artist and Maker and managed to hold on to and pass on many of the traditional practices of her people to our People, despite the forces that attempted to deny her of that right." Stokely took a few steps over and guided Yren to yet another tree. "And this is her husband, Arnaud Lemieux. He was... a complicated man, of French-Canadian ancestry. He was poor, but hardworking. It made him bitter, mean, and unpredictable. He felt he had been cheated out of his rightful place of power. He felt his whiteness should afford him certain privileges, but when the system all fell down around them not even whiteness protected Arnaud Lemieux."

"Whiteness?" Yren was a bit confused.

"A concept from the Old World, that the colour of one's skin – it's lightness – implied superiority."

Yren frowned, suspiciously.

Stokely couldn't help but to laugh at Yren's indignation. "I know. It doesn't make much sense. But it was a fairly pervasive way of thinking, and it had some very, very real consequences for people who look like you and me. There is a long, ugly history of injustices enacted upon people simply because of the colour of their skin."

"That's terrible."

"Yes. Yes, it is." Stokely watched concern consume Yren's face. "But our people – Black and Brown people, queer and gender non-conforming people – we are endlessly creative. We are persistent, and we are defiant. In my great grandmother's time it was a radical act just to claim that a Black life mattered, that its value was equal to that of someone who was white. She rallied in the streets of this land's great cities for justice. As her great grandmother before her rallied for equality during the Civil Rights Era. Because her great grandmother worked the land of another man's family, enslaved; because her people were still not free. Never doubt that profound change is possible. With time, and intention. I believe the Universe moves – always – toward Balance, in the direction of Love, in favour of Justice. The first People of the Village believed this. So that when it was clear the Old World they had known was about to fall away, they were prepared. In the ashes of the Old World, Ife planted the seeds. And the People remain to help those seeds grow."

"Asé," Yren whispered.

"Blessed be," Stokely replied.

She placed a gentle hand on Yren's chin and lifted their gaze to their own. "Injustice of that magnitude was unfathomable. I'm grateful that you, child of the New World, will never know what that was like."

Yren smiled, shyly. "Tell me more? About my family, I mean."

"Of course. Well, let's see. Irène and Arnaud came to the Village as a couple, in the latter days of the Fall, from one of the neighbouring logging towns. I'd say that more than half of the structures in the Village could not have been built without the hands and the knowledge of Arnaud and Irène. Their children were both born here, Jean and his sister Vivienne. When she was old enough, Vivienne started a family of her own with a young man named Caster Freeman. Freeman was a Black and Mi'kmaw person from the Acadia First Nation. That story is one of the oldest and most profound examples of solidarity between Black and Indigenous peoples in this land. The union between Caster and Vivienne continued that spirit of solidarity. Your being here on this land today is the embodiment of that solidarity. It is a joy and a marvel to be celebrated."

Yren allowed Stokely's words to wash over them, like a warm hug from their ancestors. Then came an intrusive thought. "But not everyone felt that way, did they?"

"You're a very perceptive child, Yren Stone." Stokely shook her head, searching for the right words. They moved over to a nearby bench and sat down.

"Elder Jean's father, Père Lemieux was... disappointed. He felt his daughter was marrying beneath her worth. In his mind he had given her the gift of whiteness, if she claimed it, despite her mother's blood. He couldn't understand why she'd choose a partner of Freeman's lineage. To Père Lemieux, Indigeneity was 'less-than'; Blackness was 'less-than'. He was consumed by the foolish, oppressive, and violent notion of superiority. You see, the mindset of the colonizer is to control, to assimilate, to eradicate the other. Père Lemieux trusted that his children would carry on those values, ally themselves with white supremacy. Vivienne made a different choice. It created a rift in their family, in your family. And while Vivienne rebelled early, it took Jean... some time to stand up to his father, to unlearn the things he'd learned. There's a bit of mistrust there still, between your Unti and Elder Jean."

Yren was quiet, absorbing the words of Elder Quay.

"You find it sad, don't you?"

Yren puzzled it over in their mind a few more moments before responding, "No. I find it... hateful. It's –"

"Enraging."

Yren bristled. *Rage.* Yes, the feeling it evoked in Yren was rage.

Elder Quay nodded solemnly. A knowing smile crept across her face. "You have a highly developed sense of justice, Yren. Follow that. I believe it will serve you well.

"Injustice should disquiet us. Try not to let it discourage you. Instead, let it motivate you into correct action. That anger that you feel about injustice can be productive. It can be creative, rather than destructive. Do not let it turn inward, upon yourself. We need not shrink ourselves because someone else's imagination cannot comprehend our full humanity. You are whole; you are worthy, and you are glorious."

Yren's smile broadened as they met the gaze of Elder Quay. At the back of their head, the tether pulsed. It sent a series of euphoric ripples along Yren's spine. Yren stared into Stokely's eyes, awestruck. "How do you know all of this?"

Stokely chuckled. "It's my vocation as a Keeper, to collect the stories of the People so that they may be passed down from one generation to the next." Stokely pointed out other white-robed figures passing between the rows, tending to the trees. "As it is also their vocation. As it one day may also be yours, should you so choose. Indeed, many of our traditions come from August and Ifedayo. It was August and Ifedayo who started the tradition of the Naming Day. As two trans people deeply in love with each other, with themselves, and the community they had helped to shape despite all obstacles, they felt it was important for every child to be celebrated for who they really were, to take a moment to honour that each and every individual is the architect of their own being."

"You are your ancestors' wildest dream." Stokely smoothed a hand across Yren's cheek. "I see so much of your mother in you. Your mother is the product of the love between Vivienne and Caster Freeman. And your mother, Dayle ... was a remarkable human being. She was a good friend to me. She would want me to remind you not to despair. No matter what challenges lay in your family history, remember *you* are here today because *love won.*" Elder Quay stood and smoothed the wrinkles from the front of her white linen tunic. She gave Yren one last knowing smile and then took her leave, gliding deeper into the sun-dappled paths of the Orchard.

Yren left with their mind and heart overflowing. There was such a rich history of people living extraordinary lives and overcoming extraordinary odds in Yren's family. It made them proud. The ongoing work of the Keepers would make it possible for future generations to visit this place and know those stories. Ama and Aba deserved to be a part of that legacy, and yet they were not. Would they be forgotten entirely in time? It wasn't fair; it wasn't right. Perhaps in time Unti would allow their trees to be planted. If only they had recovered the remains after the accident...

Lost in thought, Yren arrived on the path just outside the Orchard. They were immediately struck by a soccer ball hurtling through the air with great speed. Yren's quick reflexes managed to block it with their forearms, but the sudden impact caught Yren off-balance and knocked them over into the dirt. Yren's vision was clouded by the bright sunlight and the rising dust, but they could hear the unmistakable laughter of Jedda

Quay coming closer.

"Whoops!" Jedda cackled and her gaggle of friends joined in. "We thought you had that one for sure, Yren."

Yren still lay on the ground, brushing the dirt from their arms. One of their elbows was skinned, bleeding slightly. The tether had already begun its healing coo as it unfurled its tendrils toward the wound. Yren had a million curses waiting just behind their teeth but turned to see an open hand extended in front of their face. Augi's hand.

Though he was backlit in the sunshine, Yren could still make out the even expression on their sib's face. Augi appeared neither overly protective of Yren, nor particularly annoyed with Jedda. He simply held out his hand for Yren to take and leverage themself back onto their feet.

It was Augi's serene face that filled Yren with yet another sudden, explosive fury.

"Get away from me!"

Augi stumbled backward a few paces, visibly confused. Jedda and their laughing gang went silent. Yren stood and wiped the dust from their bottom, glaring fiercely at the assembled crowd of children. One of Jedda's minions made a move to retrieve the offending soccer ball from the ground but stopped dead at a glance from Yren.

Yren rounded back on Augi. "Were you *playing with them*?"

Augi's head tilted to one side, his ashy blond brows furrowed. Though the only words he spoke were to calmly utter Yren's name, what Yren heard and felt Augi say was *don't be so dramatic*.

"Seriously? I've just been visiting our dead parents and you're –"

"But your parents aren't in there," Jedda said plainly.

At this pronouncement, Yren and Augi both visibly winced.

"Can I have the ball back, please?"

Yren exploded. "The *ball?!*"

"Calm down, Yren." Jedda sneered, her face wrinkled with disgust. "It was an accident."

Jedda's words echoed in Yren's ears. *An accident.* Flashes of the ground crumbling beneath Ama and Aba's feet, their eyes wide in terror as they fell, their voices calling out for help. *An accident.*

Yren's breath collapsed; they felt dizzy. *Fight or flight.* They could feel the beginnings of a panic attack welling up inside. Their fists balled up into tight knots of rage. Tension gripped every fibre of Yren's body as if a white-hot current of electricity were shooting through them. At the same time an overwhelming sense of shame consumed them, amplified in the shining eyes of each of the surrounding Village kids. Yren saw their fear, their disgust, their concern and confusion.

Augi moved toward his sibling, arms outstretched. "Yren?"

"Don't touch me!"

Each member of the gang traded worried glances, and then wordlessly agreed upon retreat. Jedda snatched up the soccer ball and looked back only once to send a shrugging apology back to Augi.

"Yren, just breathe, okay?"

Every bit of Yren's spirit wanted to do anything it could to spite Augi, but in this moment it was best to concede, to breathe.

"Good. That's good. Again."

Yren choked on another set of curses. They wanted to scream *don't tell me what to do*, and yet they couldn't make a sound. Yren took another deep breath. And another. Their body relaxed; their fists opened. Yren could sense the tether sending cascading vibrations of comfort. It was as though Yren had been entirely outside of their own body, just a storm of unwieldy emotions without form. Suddenly, they were back. Yren shook out some of the remaining tension in their hands.

"Hey," Augi whispered and tried to catch Yren's gaze. "You okay?"

Wordlessly, Yren pivoted their body and began marching home. Augi stood there stunned for a few moments and then chased after them but maintained his distance. In this way, in silence, at once separate but together, the siblings made their way back to their family cabin.

Yren climbed into bed immediately, while Augi hovered in the doorway to their room. Yren stared at the ceiling, searching out patterns in the woodwork. There was the knot in the wood that looked like an owl's face. There were the swirls in the wood grain resembling a bare foot. Cataloguing these things eased Yren into drowsiness.

Their right hand hung out the side of the bed and into the centre of the room. Yren had just closed their eyes to let sleep take them when they felt Augi take their hand in his. Yren didn't open their eyes. They didn't pull their hand away.

Sometimes forgiveness doesn't come through words, but through action.

CHAPTER TWELVE

A clear sky and a white-hot sun. Thunder rumbling in the distance. And then the earth opens its mouth wide and swallows Ama and Aba right before Yren's eyes. The sandy ground crumbles beneath their feet. Their arms outstretched, their eyes wide in terror as they descend. Ama's necklace catching the light and then falling out of view.

Yren runs toward the dead tree and stops just short of the cliff's edge. They look down into the ravine. Aba's leg shattered in the fall. Don't panic, baby. Get the rope from the bag and tie one end around the tree and the other around your waist. *Yren's fingers fumbling. The sound of water rushing.*

A massive wall of grey water cuts through the narrow ravine, barrels toward Yren's parents. Then over them. Then recedes, leaving no trace of them in sight.

Panic. Intense, consuming panic. And then everything in Yren's view is washed over by a bright white light. Like staring into the sun.

A figure emerges through the fog, incredibly lean and very tall. The features of its face in shadow, but kindness. Safety. Wings? Yren counts the edges in silhouette: six massive wings. They block out the light.

A hand, outstretched.

Yren's eyes bolted open. The cabin was dark, but they could just make out the shape of the owl's face in the wooden planks in the ceiling above their bed. Another dream. Another wildly vivid and bizarre dream. Yren's brain scrambled, frantically trying to latch hold of the details before they dissipated.

The necklace. In the dark Yren fumbled out of bed to rummage through the pockets of the clothes lying in a heap beside the bed frame. They'd almost forgotten about it. They pulled free Ama's chain and the hamsa charm. She'd been wearing it the day of the accident! Yren's dream practically confirmed it. Or was their memory obscuring the truth? It made no sense for it to be in the strawberry patch. The Barrens where they'd gone that day were several kilometres further beyond the Village. What if Ama somehow ...

Yren dressed swiftly in the dark. Though they hardly made any noise, still it roused Augi.

"What are you doing?" Augi croaked from his bed.

"Going out."

Augi sat up. "Where?"

"I can't explain it." Yren shot back. "I think – I have to go see something."

Augi was having none of it. *"Go see something?"*

Yren flinched, and in a sharp whisper shot back *"Keep your voice down."* Waking Unti at this hour was not on the agenda. Yren furtively tucked the hamsa back inside their pocket and made for the bedroom door.

Augi leapt from his bed before Yren's hand reached the latch.

"Augi, what do you think you're doing?" Yren snapped.

Even in the low light Yren recognized that stern glare. It almost brought a smile to their face, thinking of how alike they were at times truly. Incredibly stubborn.

"What do you think I'm doing? I'm coming with you." Augi's face vanished for a moment as he slipped his shirt over his head.

Yren broke down. "Augi ... I have to ... I have to find them."

Augi had just pulled up his trousers but froze at these words. He seemed to choke back tears for a moment. "Their bodies, you mean."

Yren startled a little at their sibling's tone. *Their bodies.* The sound of those words coming from Augi's mouth was like an icy finger in Yren's side.

"I'm going back out to the Barrens. Alone." Yren sniffled. "I have a strange feeling. I can't explain it, Augi. I think they might be... I have to know..."

Augi stood toe to toe with his sibling, his eyes locked. Through clenched teeth he managed to eke out the words, "I'm coming with you."

"Augi it isn't safe." It wasn't a lie entirely. It wasn't safe. There were all manner of dangers in the woods outside the Village. There would be rough terrain and wild animals. They could run across a bear. Packs of wolves had exploded back into being with the diminished population of people in the world. Besides which, they would be on foot, and with Yren's abilities Yren could travel faster without Augi. Though they dared not mention it to their sibling. Alone it would be possible for Yren to get out to the Barrens and back again before anyone really took notice. With Augi along it would double, maybe even triple the time.

Augi took a few steps back and folded his arms. "Either I'm

coming with you, or I'm telling Unti."

That did it. "Fine," Yren growled back.

And with that last exchange between them, the two siblings crept quietly from their bedroom and into the common area of the cabin. They each snatched up a few supplies: food, water, the igniter to make a fire, an old LED dynamo torch to light the way. Once daylight bloomed, Augi would need his goggles to protect his sensitive eyes from the harsh sunlight of the Barrens, and his hood to protect his skin. Most summer days within the Village, children ran about in bare feet, but they would both want their heavy boots for this excursion.

Yren stood at the front door of the cabin waiting for Augi to grab the last of his things, their hand on the latch. Ready, Augi sprinted past them into the night and out the open door. Yren stood there in the doorway for a moment, looking over their shoulder in the direction of Unti's room. Yren whispered, mostly to themself but also like a little prayer, a little spell. "Back before you know it." Yren closed the door to the cabin behind them, and gently felt the latch click.

Yren descended the stairs of the decking and found Augi emerging from inside the storage shed with a length of rope in his hands. "We might need this."

Yren nodded.

Augi stuffed the rope inside his satchel, then gestured in mock formality at the path leading away from the cabin. "After you."

Yren held up a finger in pause and closed their eyes. Augi watched as they seemingly listened with their entire being for something off in the distance. A faint humming approached from the darkness above and the tether appeared, pulsing with a faint blue bioluminescence. Its wispy tendrils lilted through the atmosphere and then lay hold to the back of Yren's neck. The being reeled itself into position, as Augi had seen it do countless times before, under his sibling's big billowing hair and – he imagined – nuzzled into the dip just near the base of Yren's skull.

Yren's eyes opened, "Let's go."

They made their way along the familiar paths without the use of a torch. It was best to remain hidden until they were past the perimeter. Instead of the road past Elder Jean, Yren aimed their walk out toward the composting latrines.

"I don't suppose you know a way to get us past the clockers undetected, do you?" The tone of Augi's voice was pointed.

"I have a few ideas, yeah." Yren chuckled a little to themself.

They diverted off the path just beyond the latrines and into the brush. The perimeter of the Village, and thus a series of remote clockers that would relay the siblings' passing to whomever was on duty at the terminal in the Longhouse, lay just ahead.

"Well?" Augi chirped.

Yren gestured for Augi to be quiet. Yren crouched down low against the gnarled trunk of a massive pine tree. Augi did the same. He watched his sibling stare blankly out into the dark of the forest. There was a long silence; it made Augi nervous. Yren seemed to be calling out again voicelessly into the night.

There was movement in the brush. In the low light of the moon, Augi could just make out the shapes of a family of deer approaching. They fed absentmindedly, either not noticing the siblings huddled together nearby in the dark, or not caring.

Within a few moments Yren and Augi were surrounded.

"Stay low and move slowly," Yren commanded. "Whoever's online will just assume we're one of them."

Augi obeyed, and just that easily the siblings edged beyond the clockers and into the open wilderness. When they were clear of the perimeter, Yren's posture straightened, and they confidently stepped through the undergrowth. Augi watched as their massive hair quivered languidly, shifting as if underwater. The sprouting tendrils of the tether intensified their glow and the creature emerged from its hiding place. It began to gently glide alongside, swimming through the atmosphere, lighting the way in front of Yren.

Augi stuffed a hand roughly in his satchel, pulled out the LED torch, and clicked it on.

The darkness was expansive. Obscured by the clouds and tall trees, the moon could offer no comfort. Out here in the deep woods the black stretched on seemingly without end.

Augi had never been this far outside of the Village at night. Beyond the light of his own torch he could perceive the vague shadows of what he could only hope were trees shifting in the wind. And nothing else. Indeed, he had no idea where they were or where they were going. They had stepped willingly into the void. It was disorientating and, Augi finally admitted to himself, terrifying.

"You do that a lot?" Augi snipped.

"Do what?" Yren called back.

"Manipulate animals like that? Use your powers to sneak out?"

Yren took note of the pointed tone in Augi's voice. There was no use in trying to convince him that the herd had just magically appeared at the right moment. It would only upset him further. "I don't *manipulate* anybody. It's... a conversation."

Augi huffed audibly.

"That's not how it works, Augi. I can't force anyone to do anything they don't want to do."

"Yeah, well, I guess if you could I wouldn't be here right now, right?"

Augi was frightened, and his fear made him defensive. Yren stopped walking. They could feel Augi pull up short behind them. They turned to face their sibling. "Is this how you're planning to be on the entire trip? We've got a long way to go, you know. You might want to pace yourself." Augi's face soured. In the overarching quiet, the slightest scuffling sound jumped out from somewhere in the black. Augi startled and aimed his torch in the direction of the disturbance. His body tensed in anticipation of another noise, some encroaching beast. After a few seconds, he relaxed a little.

Yren took Augi's hand in their own. "Hey. Look at me." Augi swallowed hard and met Yren's gaze. "Just keep your eyes in the middle of my back and keep up. I won't let anything happen to you."

Yren turned swiftly on their heels and set a brisk pace, aiming them further into the black of the deep woods. Augi had a little trouble keeping up. The brush was high and the ground was uneven. He stumbled several times but kept his eyes on Yren.

"Couldn't we find a path or something?" Augi pleaded.

"The only paths this far out are game trails, Augi. You know who uses game trails, don't you?"

"Deer use game trails." Augi answered, haughtily.

"And so do the things that hunt them." Yren called back. "We're better off if we stick to the scrub, Bubs. We're less likely to run into... friends."

It occurred to Augi that they didn't appear to be following any clear path whatsoever. "How do you even know which way to go?" Augi asked meekly. "Honestly," he swatted at the branches leaping out for his face. "I can't see anything." Yren didn't answer. "Wait. Can you see in the dark? Is that, you know, like... one of your powers?"

Yren slowed their pace and glanced around in the dark night. "I hadn't given it much thought, really. But I guess. Yeah." Yren's head swivelled as they took in their surroundings more thoughtfully. The tether hovered a few metres ahead of both of them, waiting for the siblings to catch up. Yren's gaze fixed on something in the distance. "Maybe a little better than I could before."

"What is it?" Augi asked nervously.

"Nothing to be worried about, Bubs. Come on. Let's keep moving."

Yren's response only served to make Augi more anxious. "Yren," Augi whined. "How do you know the way?"

"Polaris!"

Augi was confused. "Who?"

"North Star, Augi. The Barrens are southeast, and Polaris is just back there," Yren pointed absentmindedly behind them.

Augi stared straight up into black of the night sky. It was cloudy. There wasn't a single star in sight. "But... can you see the stars *behind* the clouds?"

"Yes and no." Yren chuckled.

"Well, that doesn't make any sense! Either you can see them or you can't, Yren."

"The tether, Augi." Yren said, a little exasperated. "The tether knows where Polaris is. And if the tether knows then so do I. I don't know any other way to explain it more clearly than that, I'm sorry."

"Is that how it works?" Augi continued needling.

"Is that how *what* works?"

"Your powers? You know what the tether knows?"

"Sort of." Yren chirped. "It's hard to explain."

Augi was at his wit's end. "Try?"

The pair stopped walking. Yren knew that Augi wouldn't relent. He would needle away at Yren until he got an answer. In this particular moment, it was a way for him to occupy his fearful mind. It gave him something to focus on other than what may be lurking in the dark. Truth be told this journey into the woods was the most the siblings had spoken in months. They had each retreated into their own private worlds so completely in the time since the accident that they sometimes felt like strangers. And where Yren's abilities were concerned, they had always been encouraged to leave Augi out of it.

"It's... like an antenna. Like the radio in the Longhouse," Yren's eyes rolled. "If anyone else were still out there, I mean." Yren shook their head. "The tether... receives signals, and it sends them out. If I listen, I can tune in. I can turn up the volume on certain things."

"You mean, you can hear stuff?" Augi queried. "Or..."

"Yeah, that's part of it. But not just. It's all of my senses, Augi. Everything is... amplified. And it's not just *my* senses, I can take on the abilities of others around me." At this Augi winced a bit. "Animals, I mean. Not people, so much."

Augi's face contorted with confusion. "Does it hurt them? When you take their abilities?"

"No! Oh, no. I would never if... I don't absorb. It doesn't drain them or anything." Yren struggled to find the right words to get Augi to understand. "If anything, it's the opposite. It boosts. The tether strengthens the signal of what's already there, you see. It turns up the volume. And when I'm close enough, when I'm connected, I gain those abilities too." Yren was excited. They had never really tried to put into words for anyone else what they were capable of doing.

"So... if you were next to a squirrel right now you could, what, climb a tree? Bite through a walnut shell?"

Ouch. Yren hadn't anticipated being mocked. It was unnecessarily cruel. They watched as Augi smugly chuckled to himself.

Yren took a few measured steps toward their sibling until they stood toe to toe. "I can run. As fast as any sprinting deer. My legs don't even ache afterward." Augi's laughter ceased. Yren continued, practically growling. "I can hold my breath as long as any otter. I can see under the water, through the muck. I can smell the fish upstream. I know how far away they are just by the vibration in the current." Yren saw the smile fade from Augi's lips. "And, yes. I imagine I could climb a tree as easily as any squirrel... or crack a walnut with my jaws." Augi's face dropped completely. "Jealous?"

Augi stared at the ground shamefully. "I'm sorry."

Yren took off at a clip toward the tether waiting in the distance.

"Yren!" They didn't respond. "Yren, I'm sorry." Augi stood and watched Yren barrelling stubbornly through the brush. He called out once more. "You *know* I'm jealous!" At this admission, Yren stopped. Augi continued, "I've always been jealous."

Augi took a few careful steps toward his fuming sibling. "You got to be the special one. It was like they barely even saw me anymore after a while. First you were sick and I had to stay away. Then those... *things* came and I had to stay away. And you were always running off into the middle of the woods with Ama and Aba. And they always made up some excuse to leave me behind and –"

"It was to *protect you*, Augi! It wasn't safe! Not when I was sick and not afterward when... they were only ever trying to keep you out of danger! They loved you. Ama and Aba didn't want you around me because they weren't sure if..." Yren could feel the tears welling up. "They thought *I* might be dangerous." Yren crouched down sobbing, sending the contents of their satchel spilling out into the dirt.

Augi extended a hand to stroke Yren's back, but they brushed him off. "Don't, Augi." The guilt was almost too much. Was this it? Was this the moment Yren finally told their sibling the true

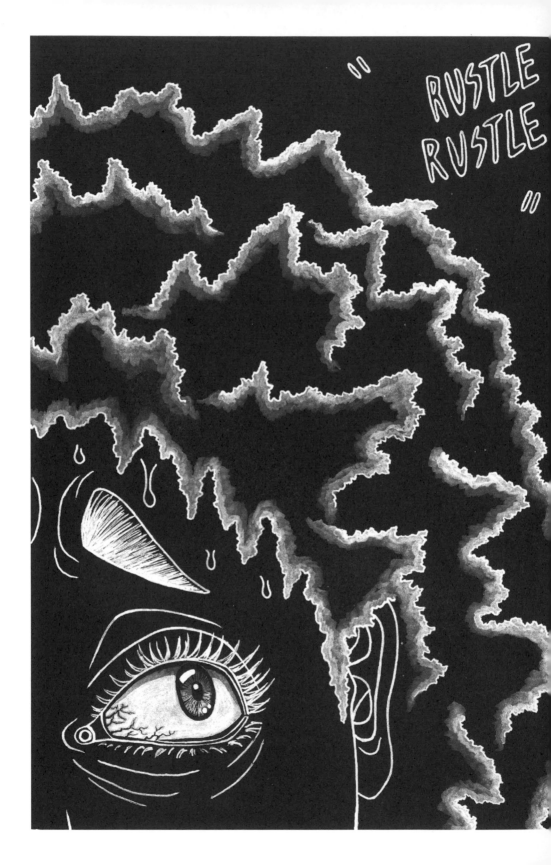

cause of the accident?

"Or what, you're gonna crunch me up like a walnut?"

Yren couldn't help but to laugh. Augi gently soothed Yren's back and shoulders with his free hand. The other aimed the LED torch into the darkness. There came another rustling sound from somewhere in the blackness.

"Hey, Yren." Something in Augi's voice had changed. "I think we've got company."

Yren sprang upright and peered intently in the direction of the beam of light from Augi's torch. A few short metres away, two gleaming yellow eyes reflected back the torchlight. There was an ominous chittering sound as the beast stopped short and stood up to its full height on its hind legs. It glared directly at the two of them.

"Do you think it's hungry?" Augi whispered.

"Starving," Yren replied.

The creature dropped down on all fours and lumbered toward them, completely unafraid. Its massive, furry body swayed back and forth. The siblings took a few cautious steps backward. They watched as a set of slinky, black claws snapped up a handful of the spilled jerky from the dust in front of Yren's feet. Then the raccoon sat back on his chubby bum and began munching, tittering gleefully.

"Friend of yours?"

"We've met before." Yren smirked. "But I wouldn't go so far as to call us friends."

The tether gracefully swooped in from Yren's left side and tickled the back of Yren's neck with its tendrils. It nestled itself into the space at the back of Yren's head and began pulsing softly.

"Is it amplifying the raccoon's abilities?" Augi asked, excitedly.

Yren laughed. "I don't think a healthy appetite is necessarily a superpower, Bubs."

"Fair point," Augi chuckled back. "I am a little hungry though."

"Why don't we rest for a bit? Get something in our bellies." Augi nodded in agreement. Yren swiped a hand across their own face. It was a bit tight from the tears that had dried there. "Think you can gather up some kindling? I'll build us a little pit for a fire."

"Sure thing," said Augi. He shone his light on the forest floor and started picking up dead branches while Yren arranged a small, neat stone circle to contain the fire. Within a few moments the siblings had a small fire going. Yren and Augi warmed themselves against the early morning chill. There was no light in the sky as yet, but it would not be much longer before the birds began to sing. They filled their bellies with snacks and water, sharing what they'd brought along with their new furry friend.

In the glow of the firelight the darkness diminished. With their bellies full of food the tension seemed to lift. Their raccoon companion had curled his body into a plump little ball and lay with his bum warming by the fire.

"This is nice," Augi said drowsily, his eyes suddenly heavy. "I'm sorry I was such a jerk earlier. Thanks for bringing me."

Yren nodded absentmindedly. They had lost themself in thought, travelled to another memory, staring into the heart of the fire. This is how it started, with Yren and Ama and Aba, gathered around a small fire, out in the wilds...

Don't be afraid. We're here to protect you if anything goes wrong. We're safe, way out here. No one is going to get hurt, baby, we promise. Just concentrate on what you're doing.

"Augi?"

"Yeah, Yren?"

"There's something more I should tell you... about the day of the accident."

CHAPTER THIRTEEN

Yren watched Augi's face go slack through the licking flames of the campfire between them. Yren felt their chest tighten, their stomach drop. This was a conversation they had never intended to have with their sibling. Yet it seemed the moment had arrived.

"I know that... we kept things from you to protect you. But you deserve to know –"

"You don't have to do this, Yren. You don't have to talk about it. I was there watching the day the news reached the Council. I heard everything you said to them already."

"You... what?"

"I was listening. Just like when I brought you up with me to see Elder Jean and Unti fighting over that gun or whatever it was you found."

Yren sat there blinking, a little stunned.

Augi continued. "You and Ama and Aba took off that morning and left me with Unti again. I was mad about it, of course. He tried to keep me busy in his studio. I made a few clay figurines and then got bored, so I asked if I could go out to play. Maybe that's why no one came looking for me?

"You were so out of it that day. When you stumbled back into the Village alone, crying. It didn't take long for a crowd to gather... and they took you to the Council. Unti rushed to the Longhouse. Everyone was so worried about you that no one noticed me. I climbed up the drainpipe. I like to watch them, the Council. I learn things. Gossip in the Village... the things that people don't say." Here Augi paused in the telling of his story to pat the bum of the sleeping racoon beside them. "You said the earth had swallowed them. That a great big hole had opened up in the dunes, made a crack in the land." Augi took a deep breath before he continued. "You said Aba had broken his leg in the fall. So you tied a rope around your waist, and the other end to a tree, to try and help them out. But then the water came. A big wall of dirty water. And it washed over them. And when it receded... they were gone." Augi looked at Yren with tears in his eyes. "You see. I know. No one had to tell me anything."

Yren's face went hot, either from the fire or with shame, they could not tell.

"I know more than you think I know. I know more than maybe even you." Augi's expression was strange. His voice was distant, cold.

Yren was shaken. "What do you mean, Bubs?" The tether, which had been gliding around the encampment in languid circles, pulsating and glowing, reached out for Yren and took up its usual hiding place at the nape of their neck, within the nest of Yren's voluminous afro.

"The first morning after those... things got here. The tethers. I was out of the house, staying with Unti. They kept us separated back then. Remember? They were afraid I'd get sick too, I guess. We were just babies, but I was already... jealous. Ya know? They always made such a fuss over you. That morning, when the Council meeting was called together... and all the elders from the Fifteen Families ran off, including Unti... I followed. That was the first time I watched. No one even noticed me." Augi chuckled, dryly. "People were scared that day. The Council thought about killing the tethers. They thought about killing the people they were attached to too. Did you know that?"

"What?" Yren's head was spiralling.

"Yeah. I heard it for myself. I think maybe that's when I decided to keep up my secret visits to the Council. I think they might have actually done it too, if it weren't for Aba. He said he couldn't do it. He said he –"

"He had already tried." The memory leapt up in front of Yren like a pouncing animal. "He had an axe in his hands when I first woke up that morning. I'd had a fever for weeks; I was delirious. I don't remember much from that time. But I remember that."

"Aba told the Council the tether had cured you. They decided to let things play out. It didn't take long for other folks to get better too. Better than better. Healthier than before, stronger than before. Some people even with abilities like you!"

"Not like me."

Augi shot a puzzled look at his sib.

"I haven't met anyone yet who can do the things that I can do." Yren stared into the palms of their own hands. "Maybe it would have been better if Aba had –"

"Don't. Don't even. Ama and Aba loved us; they *loved you*. I don't think Aba would ever have done anything to harm you. And they definitely tried to make up for it. All your special picnics out here in the wilds. Without me. It's awful what happened that day. But, I know you did your best to save them, Yren. It's not your fault."

"That's just it, Augi. I think... I think it might be." Yren was overwhelmed. "You know the story I told the Council. But that's not the whole story." Yren braced themself. "Let me show you something that might help you understand."

Yren gazed deeply into the fire. At the base of Yren's neck the tether began to quiver. First, Yren saw the shape in their mind's eye, and then the fire obeyed. Augi watched in awe as the flames condensed into a perfect sphere, then morphed slowly into a pyramid of pure, radiant light before they evaporated back into their natural, familiar state.

"What... what was that?"

"That was me."

"You told me... you didn't manipulate things. You said you couldn't make anything do what it didn't want to!"

"I... I can't! Not really. At least, I don't think so. I mean... I can shape the flames because on some level they're a part of me. Of all of us. I guess."

Augi glared at Yren suspiciously.

Begrudgingly, Yren went on. "It started... the first autumn after the tethers had come. I was in the common room, sitting by the fire. You were already sleeping. Ama was scribbling out some lesson plan for school the next day. Aba was tinkering with one of his contraptions. Just a normal night. I remember feeling so warm, so happy.

"I was looking into the fire and... I don't know, it just sort of happened. I reached out without thinking and took some of the flames into my hand. Just like that. Like it was the most natural thing in the world to do. Ama saw first, yelled out. It broke my concentration and the fireball leapt back into the fireplace. Ama and Aba both ran over, checking my hands. But I wasn't burned. I wasn't burned."

Yren held up their right hand and never breaking their gaze from their sibling, plunged it into the fire. Augi gasped, startled a little. But when Yren pulled back their hand and turned it over he could clearly see Yren was uninjured.

"They were so mad at me, absolutely furious... asking me what I was thinking, reaching into the fire like that. And I think... a little scared. Of me. Of what I may be capable of. They kept a close watch on me after that. They made me promise not to do it again. And they sent you away a lot, to be with Unti, to keep you safe... from me.

"Deep winter came, and all the Fifteen Families moved to bunk in the Longhouse. Elder Jean had Story at his side constantly. He was just a little thing back then, remember? A real live wolf cub! It was like... wow. Jean's tether had already come and gone, but the connection it left behind between Jean and Story was so powerful. Elder Jean was always so gentle with Story; and Story just adored Jean, you could tell. It made all the kids so happy to have Story around that winter. Elder Jean used to tell me that, in time, maybe I would discover my heightened abilities through my tether as well. I think it was seeing the connection between Story and Jean that helped convince Ama and Aba to let me test out my abilities.

"That spring was our first trip out to the Barrens. I was terrified. But Ama and Aba said everything would be okay, way out there. The soil in the Barrens is already so alkaline, so sandy, that hardly anything grows there... except for the pines. Fires happen out there all the time; there are huge fields of burnt out trees and shrubs, and big clearings for kilometres in all directions. That's why they would take me way out there. In a big stretch of barren land like that there'd be no harm done. If anything caught fire by mistake it would become part of the natural features of the land. The perfect training grounds.

"For me, I learned, all things seemed rooted first in our connection to this Earth. I can dig my hands into the soil and feel the forces coming together. The tether amplifies the signal and... I could call the animals, and they would come. I could shape the fire, and not be burned. Ama and Aba thought that maybe my abilities had other *elemental properties*. That's how Ama put it. I think they got to a point where it didn't frighten them anymore; it excited them. It excited *us*! We tried water a few times. I could swim well enough, but always had to come up for air eventually. Though I could shape it, like the fire. Same for the earth, if I tried, if I concentrated. The grains of sand would swell up from the dunes and collapse into simple shapes... a pyramid, a ball, a cube. After a few years, Aba thought maybe it was time to challenge me a bit more."

The expression on Augi's face darkened. Yren could see it for themself. They went on with their story. "Sand was the obvious choice. It responded quickly and went back to its natural form without much fuss. There was less danger than spending hours in the river or playing with fire, we thought." Yren's throat went dry and they tried to choke back a bit of saliva in order to continue. "That day in the Barrens, Aba wanted me to try to manifest more complicated shapes. *Think of home. Show me the Longhouse*, he said. *Just like building a sandcastle, but with your mind. Just concentrate on what you're doing*, they said. My hands were dug down into the sand. I could feel the energy building and then... the strangest thing happened, Augi. I could sense it coming but... it was *different* somehow. It was... something outside of me, and I couldn't stop it, couldn't control it! And then –"

Augi stood. "And then the ground opened up... and swallowed our parents?"

Tears streamed down Yren's face as they looked up at their sibling. The first glimmers of sunrise crept over the horizon. The birds had begun to sing cheerfully, and yet here they both were, heartbroken.

Before either of them could speak another word, a resonant howl rang out across the wilderness. The chubby raccoon awoke and ran off, scrabbling up a nearby tree.

"Wolves. Let's move!"

A second, answering call rang out through the wilderness. It was louder and closer than the first. They worked together to smother the fire, packed up whatever belongings lay scattered on the ground, and made quick time through the woods in the direction of the Barrens.

"When you love someone,
you say their name
different.
Like it's safe
inside your mouth."

- Jodi Picoult

CHAPTER FOURTEEN

With the approaching dawn the forest came alive, and there was movement everywhere in the dimly lit corners of the wilds. A patchy fog descended. It obscured the view as the siblings stumbled bravely forward. Leaves rustled in the shivering brush; pebbles skittered across the ground. Was that a sparrow streaking across the inky blue sky or a bat? Did a chipmunk just dash along the forest floor, or was that a viper slithering through the dried pine needles? All of creation was clambering to meet the dawn, all creatures great and small. The effect was far from a feeling of safety. The shift was a reminder that danger potentially lay behind every patch of scrub, within the crags of every bit of darkly looming boulder. The siblings had made it safely through the night. Would they also survive the day?

Both Yren and Augi were on high alert. There had not been another wolf-call in some time, but it only meant that they couldn't tell just how far away the wolves may be. The pines in this section of the forest grew in dense groves, with the trees sometimes so close to one another it was as if the siblings were weaving through a crowd of people. Yren adapted, dancing swiftly from side to side. But Augi was slowing Yren down, just as they had feared before leaving the safety of the Village. He also hadn't uttered a single word since they'd left the campfire.

Ahead of them Yren could see a gap in the treeline. Rolling white clouds of fog billowed in the empty space. Yren slowed their pace, listening with their entire body. They could hear the rippling of water, the caw of crows, the gentle rush of wind. As they advanced, the landscape opened up into a marshy clearing. A shallow patch of water stretched out across the expanse of horizon, dotted with clumps of flaxen reeds. Yren could just make out a few broken, hollowed tree trunks along the banks of the water in the foggy distance. The quiet was eerie. Yren stopped short along the water's edge and peered out into the mist.

"What is it?" whispered Augi.

Yren didn't want to admit it outright, but they had never seen this place before. Not that they could remember. Not like this at least. They were lost. Yren must have made a wrong turn somewhere, lost in their own head worrying about Augi's reaction to Yren's news about the accident and the possibility of an encroaching pack of wolves.

Augi's voice trembled from behind "Yren? What is it?"

"I'm just... a little turned around is all, Bubs."

"What?!" Augi's voice echoed across the clearing.

In the distance a crow called out and took to the air. Yren raised a hand, a signal to hush their sibling. The tether, at first dormant, sent a pulse of warning down Yren's spine. "Augi... there's something out there."

A howl echoed through the air, closer than any of the others had been before. Without thinking, Augi silently crept forward and grasped Yren's left arm. He was trembling. "We need to keep moving, Bubs." Yren took a moment to get their bearings, then resolutely aimed them both southward. "It's this way." Yren held their right arm out in front of them for balance while Augi clung to their left side. Together like that they moved over the uneven ground and slipped further into the consuming blanket of fog.

A few steps in, their feet hit cold, shallow water. Yren had a choice to make. They could either wade further into the marsh, perhaps waist-high or more at its deepest, or they could detour around the water's edge. Through the water would be the direct route, but Yren couldn't put Augi through that. He would surely panic. Keeping their sib calm helped Yren to keep calm themself. One step at a time, Yren led Augi around the water's edge.

Something was moving in the water. There was a steady rippling sound growing louder, growing closer, just off to Yren's right side. Yren squinted up their eyes, searching for a discernible shape on the water's surface. *Let it be something harmless that would make sense of the noise*, Yren thought. Perhaps a duck bobbing along peacefully, or a beaver hard at work pushing a log across the water. But the shape was much bigger than a beaver. And it was heading toward the land a few metres directly in front of them.

A massive shadow emerged from within the mist. Yren and Augi stood and watched as water cascaded down its hair-covered body. Over two metres tall at its shoulder and weighing well over a thousand pounds, it was easily the biggest living thing either of the siblings had ever laid eyes on. The bull moose shook the water from its body, the colossal crown of its antlers swinging dangerously back and forth. Spanning nearly two metres from tip to tip, the antlers had yet to begin shedding for the rutting season. They were still covered in a layer of soft brown velvet; the edges were still rounded. In a month or so this layer would fall off, leaving behind a thorny crown of bloody bone. He would be a gruesome creature indeed when that time came.

Augi clung to Yren's side while Yren began to calculate their options. It was late summer; the evenings had already begun to grow cooler. Was it too early or was this just the beginning of the rutting season? All over the wilderness bulls would soon begin competing against one another, testing their strength in vicious battles. During this time the bulls were short-tempered, quick to react, eager for a fight. The bull might consider their presence a threat, a challenge to his own strength. He would feel a need to prove himself.

Yren whispered back at Augi, "Stay very still, and don't make a sound."

The bull took a few more steps out of the marsh, his lean powerful legs thundering against the ground as he walked. Out of the corner of his eye he had caught sight of Yren and Augi almost immediately but appeared unbothered. The sibling's best chance of survival was for the moose to entirely overlook them. If he decided to charge no force on earth could stop him. Yren glanced skillfully over the bull's body looking for signs of tension or aggression. Were his nostrils flared? Were his ears back? Were his hackles bristling at attention?

The moose stuck its bulbous muzzle deep into the nearby reeds and began grazing absentmindedly. The rack of his antlers crushed the foliage as he moved along. Yren exhaled, the tension in their shoulders released. Augi's fingers, once dug in tight to Yren's forearm, began to relax.

"Just back up slowly, okay Bubs? Let's give him a little space to move on his way."

Yren heard the gentle footfalls of their sibling edging backward, felt the space growing between them, and then took a few steps back themself to close the gap. They managed to ease back gracefully, increasing the distance between themself and imminent danger. Then another sound reached Yren's ears – a low, rumbling growl in the treeline behind them.

The hunched figure slunk forward, moving low to the ground. The rumbling growl grew closer and closer. Augi's ragged breathing hit Yren squarely on the cheek, and his grasp had tightened once again. Neither of the siblings turned to face the wolf directly. Augi was paralyzed with fear; Yren kept their eyes squarely on the bull moose.

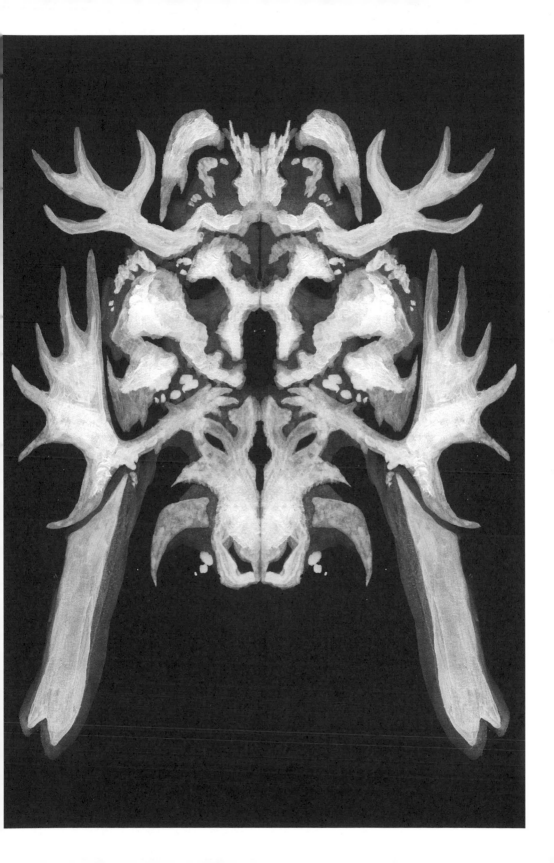

The tether lit up with a brilliant bioluminescent glow. Its limbs began to palpate excitedly. Yren couldn't understand at first what was happening as a strange feeling of happiness washed over them. *Familiarity*.

"Stand down," Yren commanded, as the great grey wolf advanced further forward, its enormous white teeth flashing. "I said, *stand down*."

Yren locked eyes on Story. He must have been trailing them this entire time, all the way from the Village! If Story was here with them, then surely the siblings' absence had been noticed – if not yet by Unti then at least by Elder Jean. If they made it out of this moment alive, Yren thought to themself, a whole new kind of danger awaited them at home now that they had been discovered.

Story would not be swayed. The wolf continued edging forward in an effort to put himself between the cowering siblings and the towering moose. It was the wolf's intention to protect the siblings at all costs. The bull moose craned his thick neck out of the brush, then slowly turned his massive body to face the three of them. There had been a moment where a confrontation could have been avoided, where they could have escaped unnoticed. That moment had passed. The bull huffed twice and bobbed his head to flash the intimidating rack of his antlers. The situation would swiftly spiral out of control if something more could not be done. Yren's mind shuffled through a million different, deadly scenarios.

Yren crouched down low and dug their fingers deep into the damp, gritty earth beneath them. The tether pulsed, its tendrils undulating Yren's hair as it began broadcasting. Eyes closed, Yren focused all their intention first on Story. Augi watched the ears of the great grey wolf relax from their posture of attack. Story sat back obediently, still at attention, but no longer ready to lunge.

"Yren... it's working."

Next, the moose. Yren opened their eyes and stared the massive bull down. He was agitated, huffing aggressively. His right hoof rose up and stamped down sharply, sending up a spray of mud across his shuddering, muscled chest. The moose bowed his head low, displaying his broad antlers in attack position. Yren could feel his power radiating outward, amplified in the connection to the tether. Yren's own muscles swelled in response. Their hair began dancing wildly, adrenaline coursing through their veins.

The bull made his mind up in an instant. With an explosive flash of strength, he began his deadly charge. Time slowed as Yren watched his powerful legs send sprays of mud hurtling into the air. A wall of bone came barreling toward them. From behind them Yren felt Augi collapse to his knees in terror. Story crouched down and prepared to strike. Yren shut their eyes tight, their hands still buried deep in the earth, bracing for impact.

A sound like an explosion, a tremendous shockwave of energy rattled the ground. A chasm two metres wide and three metres deep opened up in the space between the moose and the siblings. The bull moose stopped short of the gap, peddled itself backward. Slipping in the mud, the moose just managed to avoid falling in. He huffed angrily twice more, turned his bulky frame in the direction of the woods, and trotted off.

Yren lay back in the mud, exhausted. Story licked at their face, his tail wagging frantically. Augi flung himself on top of Yren in an embrace. Yren hugged him back, then slowly sat up. The two burst out laughing uncontrollably, overcome with relief.

"Let's... not do that again?"

Augi shook his head. "Yeah, no. Let's not." Augi wiped some mud from the side of his cheek with the back of his hand and then glanced over at Story. "What do we do about him?"

Story continued licking mud and a bit of blood from a small scrape on Yren's chin. Yren chuckled and gently pushed Story back. "Well, they must know we're gone. There's no point in going back before doing what we came out here for," Yren sighed resolutely. "Story comes with us! It'll be good to have some extra protection."

"Yeah. We see how well that works."

"He was only trying to help, Bubs." Yren stood up, their backside was covered in mud. Their muscles ached, and they felt a little wobbly. Yren's eyes tracked over the chasm in the ground in front of them. They had acted on instinct; the use of their powers had been more like an automatic reflex than anything with intent. It was unnerving. Someone could have gotten hurt. The effort had been draining. It took a few moments for Yren to regain their strength. The early morning fog had burned off and the day was bright and new. Yren took a deep breath of the morning air and turned to Augi. "Let's keep going. It's not much further now."

The tether floated ahead guiding the way. Another hour went by and gradually the muddy ground of the marsh subsided and became more coarse, more sandy. The trees grew thinner and further between as they walked. Yren got excited. From the change in the landscape Yren knew they had finally reached the edge of the Barrens. First they would pass through a scorched section of forest, littered with the remains of charred trees but bursting back to life with low-blooming flowers. Then the pines would drop away entirely, opening up on an almost desert-like space. Here only a few dead trees would dot the horizon, but

Yren need only recognize one – the dead tree on the edge of the sinkhole where Ama and Aba went down.

Yren was tired, but eager to arrive at their destination. They stopped for a moment to catch their breath. Without looking, Yren stuck a hand inside their satchel, fishing around for water. Their fingers grazed Ama's necklace before pulling the canteen out and putting it to their lips.

Without much cover overhead, Augi had opted to slip on his googles. Though it was early in the day, the sun was much stronger out near the Barrens than at home in the Village. It was because of the goggles that Yren hadn't noticed Augi had been crying. It was only when he lifted the goggles to search his own pack that Yren caught sight of their siblings' tears.

"Bubs?"

Augi looked up from his bag and wiped his eyes. He gave a weak little smile.

"Augi, what's wrong?"

"Nothing. It's just... thank you."

"For what?"

"Yren... you just saved our lives! All of us!" Augi nodded in the direction of Story, who'd taken the stop as an opportunity to flop down in the shadow of a stump. Yren watched him roll over on his back, his pink tongue drooping from one side of his jaws, drooling happily on a small clump of trillium and clover.

"I just did what I could, Bubs. If I had been able to do more we wouldn't be out here now."

Augi searched out a little patch of shade and flopped down on the ground. He wrestled his canteen from his satchel and took a few measured sips of water. He was quiet for a moment. He looked up at Yren. "I know you didn't do it on purpose. I know you didn't mean to... I know it was an accident."

Yren felt a knot relax in their stomach. They'd been waiting since the campfire for Augi to say something, anything, about the accident. Blame or forgiveness, it didn't really matter, as long as Augi didn't pretend like nothing was ever said.

Yren took a seat on the ground next to their sib. The tether continued swimming through the air just above their heads. "Thank you. You know, I haven't done anything quite like what I did back there since the accident. I've been too afraid. Too ashamed."

"Yeah. I can understand that." Augi folded in on himself a little, lost in thought.

"I shouldn't have kept these things from you, Augi. It was wrong, and I'm sorry. I know we haven't always gotten along so well, especially since... since we lost Ama and Aba. But I hope you know I love you. You know that, right? I will always do my best to defend you. And I don't want to keep anything from you. You're the person I trust most in this world! I don't ever want to betray your trust in me."

Augi was quiet for a long while, staring off into space and playing with a bit of the rope from the storage shed. "I'm sorry too," he sighed.

"So, no more secrets then? From here on out, we'll always be honest with each other." Yren stuck out their hand for Augi to shake. Augi hesitated.

"Yren... do you remember the day you came home with that fracking cannon or whatever it is?"

Yren's face flushed hot. The day Yren had found that cannon was the day they'd also found what they still felt in their heart was Ama's hamsa necklace. But how could that be? It was foolish to think so, wasn't it? That necklace was the reason Yren had to come back out to the Barrens to search for the remains of their parents. If Yren and Augi could just find their parents' remains then maybe Yren could finally let go of hope. And Ama and Aba could join their rightful place with the rest of their ancestors in the Orchard of the Dead. After the guilt, it was the foolish hope that Ama and Aba may still be alive that ate away the most at Yren. It was stupid to hope. It made Yren feel childish, powerless. If they were alive why wouldn't they have just come home? Wouldn't they have tried to make their way home? No, that necklace was a false hope. It would be cruel to show it to Augi, whether they had just sworn to no more secrets or not. Yren had already done enough damage.

All of these thoughts raced through Yren's mind in an instant. The look on their face must have been one of total panic, but Augi didn't seem to notice. He looked a little sickly himself.

"Remember you came to the shed?"

"Yeah," Yren managed. "Yeah, I was looking for that rope. I was gonna hide the cannon in the cistern by the compost toilets. I was gonna use the rope to tie it off and hang it from the grate but –"

"But I was in the shed already."

Yren chuckled. "Yeah!"

"With Jedda."

Yren sat there in a stunned silence for a few moments. "With... *Jedda?*"

Augi sat with his arms hugging his knees. "Yeah. Remember Jedda dragged me off to dance at her Naming Day? Well, we sort of... started hanging out together more after that. That's where I've been when I'm not around. I've been with Jedda." Augi hung his head, staring at the ground between his feet.

Yren's back straightened, their mouth hung agape. "So you two are like friends or something now? You're a part of her... crew of bullies or whatever?"

Augi glared back at Yren. "They're just other kids, Yren. And Jedda's not as bad as you make her out to be. She can be really nice if you just give her a chance."

"Oh, please," Yren huffed. "Jedda's a brat and a bully. And she probably just latched on to you to get back at me!"

"What?!" Augi's eyes went wide.

"For not liking her back. She's been after me for ages, always touching me and trying to –"

Augi stood up suddenly, his fists clenched. "You take that back!"

Yren stood up to meet Augi's gaze. "Bubs, you're being silly. Just because you've been –" here Yren pretended to wretch, for emphasis, *"making out* in the storage shed or whatever else with *Jedda Quay* for a few weeks doesn't change anything. You don't think Jedda actually *likes* you, do you?"

"And why wouldn't she?"

Yren paused and took a deep breath. Their words had obviously stung. "That's... not how I meant it, Bubs."

"Oh, how did you mean it?"

Yren stammered for a few seconds. "I... I..."

"I don't wanna talk about it anymore. Let's just go!" Augi turned on his heels and marched deeper into the Barrens.

"Augi, wait!" Yren called. "Bubs! I'm sorry! It's just... *Jedda Quay*."

"I SAID I DON'T WANT TO TALK ABOUT IT ANYMORE!" Augi hollered back.

Yren stooped to snatch up their satchel, tossing the strap over one shoulder. "All right, all right. We don't have to talk about it anymore." Story, who'd stopped rolling in the dirt some time ago, cocked his head to one side and stared at Yren. "Come on, Story. Let's go."

Yren kept their distance, letting Augi take the lead. They hadn't meant to hurt Augi's feelings, but the idea of Augi and Jedda even being friends, let alone *kissing*, was repulsive to Yren. The idea of trying to make Augi feel better about his admission was even more repulsive. There was a knot in Yren's stomach over it, a mix of betrayal and – if they were really being honest with themself – a little jealousy. Yren didn't even like Jedda, but they had grown used to *being liked*. No, no... the whole situation was just too bizarre.

Meanwhile, Story trotted between the two of them happily, occasionally licking at the inside of one of Yren's palms as they walked or gently nipping at one of Augi's fingers. A short time later the forest gave way completely to a wide expanse of flat, hot earth and open sky.

Augi stopped walking and pointed to a dead, grey tree a short distance away. "That's it, isn't it?"

Yren came up alongside Augi and nodded. "That's it."

CHAPTER FIFTEEN

Without another word between them Yren, Augi, Story and the tether took off at speed toward the dead tree. There was so little variation to the landscape, and so little elevation to the horizon that the chasm was not at first obvious. As they grew closer they could see the edge of the giant hole that had opened up in the earth.

"This is where they went in." Yren whispered quietly, as they all stared down into the pit.

The sinkhole was at least ten metres across in all directions and had to be at least twice that deep. The sandy soil on the sides easily crumbled away at the touch. Yren knelt down and with one hand grasping the trunk of the dead tree for balance, they scooped up a handful of earth in their free hand. It collapsed almost immediately into dust. It confirmed what Yren already knew, they could not have climbed out on their own.

Augi scanned the horizon with his eyes. "Yren this doesn't seem right. This hole... it's huge!"

Yren stood and wiped the dust from their palms. "Yeah?"

"Well, it took almost everything you had in you to make a hole less than half this size earlier."

"Yeah?"

"And you said there was water, right? Ama and Aba got washed away by a wall of dirty water, that's what you said."

Yren wasn't quite following; they were a bit annoyed. "I wasn't lying! That's exactly what happened, just like I told you!"

"I never said that you were lying! I'm just saying, it was all just an idea before. But now, now that I've seen what your power can do, this... this doesn't seem... *like you*. I'm not being mean, I swear I'm not, but I don't think you have enough power for this. And – "

Yren's shoulders relaxed, their jaw unclenched.

Augi continued. "And the water, Yren. You can't make something out of nothing. It's like a desert out here! It doesn't make any sense. Where did the water come from?"

Yren followed Augi's gaze to the other side of the chasm. There they could see a fissure, a great big crack in the earth. Yren pointed across the divide. "There. The water came from there."

Augi and Yren took off running around the edge of the sinkhole with Story and the tether following behind. When they reached the lip of the fissure the siblings slowed their pace. "They must have been washed back this way," Augi reasoned. "Sucked back with the receding water through this gap." The crack wasn't nearly as wide as the sinkhole itself. It was actually quite narrow, only a few metres across in some sections, and Story leapt easily from one side of the gap to the other. But it was long, stretching on and on into the distance.

They had walked at least another hour along the ledges of the fissure, peering down constantly, searching for anything noteworthy. Turkey vultures circled overhead, on the lookout for flesh to scavenge. Yren wondered how many meals the vultures had managed to claim from this desert. Any creature that wandered out here would be foolish to do so. If this land had ever been green once, that was a long time ago. Yren could not spot even a tree for kilometres in any direction. The ground beyond the fissure was parched, cracked clay. Gusts of wind sent up clouds of dust. The heat was sweltering. Story was panting heavily. Augi had draped his protective cape over his head and shoulders, secured his goggles to his sweating face. Even the tether seemed to tire in the hot sun and went to burrow in the shade and safety of Yren's hair. Yren wiped the sweat from their brow with the back of their forearm. They took another swig of water from the nearly empty canteen before pouring a bit in their hand for Story, and then passing the rest of the canteen to Augi to finish.

"This is bizarre, Yren. I don't get it. We should have found... something by now."

"We should keep going, Bubs. When the hunters came out to scout this area after the accident they wouldn't have come as far out as we have now. Let's at least see where this leads. If we can find the source of the water then maybe we can –"

"Yren? What is that?"

Yren and Augi had been scanning the bottom of the fissure all this time, not bothering to keep an eye on the horizon. After all, the land was flat and featureless for as far as the eye could see. It was no wonder they hadn't yet spotted it. In the distance there was an enormous crater in the surface of the earth. Indeed, they had only noticed it at this distance because it was so vast, so wide. It was absolutely massive, making the sinkhole seem puny by comparison. It was instantly clear to them both that the crater was the starting point of the fissure that Yren and Augi had been following all this way.

"I bet *that*," Yren said "is what we've been looking for."

Just then Story caught the scent of something on the wind. He held his wet, black nose aloft in the breeze and it twitched frantically.

"What is it, Story? What's out there?"

Story bolted, top speed, in the direction of the crater, with Yren and Augi chasing after. Within moments they were at the edge, looking down at a sight for which neither of the siblings could have prepared themselves.

"Augi, get down! Now! Story! Lie down!" Yren's commands were heeded immediately. The three of them lay flat on their stomachs in the sandy earth.

The crater descended several kilometres deep, deep, deep down into the earth. At its centre, like a jewel, sat a massive, perfectly still turquoise lake. Yren could see streaks of clouds in its reflection. From this vantage point, high above, Yren and Augi could see the crater wasn't really a crater at all. Nothing made by nature looked like this. All along its edges the earth had been packed down hard into what could only be described as a road. The road snaked down in concentric circles until it plateaued out at the bottom, level with the lake. And all along the road... were people! Hundreds of people! They were dressed from head to toe in ragged jumpsuits of dark fabric, pushing heavy carts steadily uphill, or holding bright yellow cannons like the one Yren had found that day in the wilds. These people held their cannons aimed at the earth, firing powerful streams of compressed water that sliced through the rock with ease. They were boring massive tunnels into the earth. Yren and Augi had never seen so much destruction before! Nor had they ever seen so many people: adults *and children*. There were children, no older than Yren and Augi.

"Yren, I'm scared. I think we should go."

Yren lay there in awe for another few moments, their breath bouncing back the dusty earth, their mind trying to make sense of what they were seeing. Mixed in here and there among the workers there were also others who weren't working. They wore red jumpsuits that covered their entire bodies, with broad armoured shoulders and gleaming helmets that covered their faces. It was obvious they were guards of some sort; their cannons were different. Yren strained their eyes to get a better look. They could just make out a figure in a dark jumpsuit resting for a moment against a boulder. One of the red-suited guards approached the resting worker, their weapon aimed high into the air. The guard fired two warning shots, and two white-hot pulses darted into the sky. Then the guard aimed the rifle at the worker, who quickly leapt to their feet and back to toiling.

All this time they'd believed the rest of the world had fallen away. No one in the Village had seen or heard any signs of civilization for *six years*! They thought the Plague had wiped out humanity, or at least all the humanity a person could travel to from the Village. The people of the Village had lost contact with every other group of which they had knowledge. Yren had always felt somehow that it was impossible for no one else to have survived. Now they were confronted with the sudden reality that not only had others survived but, perhaps, those that had were people to be afraid of.

"Yren?" Augi's voice was icy, sharp.

Story growls. The tether shoots a bolt of warning down Yren's spine. Yren turns in time to see two red-suited guards standing over them. No faces! Shiny helmets with black visors reflecting the light. No faces! Black leather gloves, fingers on their triggers. Yren scrambles to their feet. A flash of bright white light, and Yren's whole body goes rigid. Paralyzed, unable to move! Yren collapses on their back into the dirt. They hear Augi cry out. They hear one of the guards scream as Story lunges toward him... and then everything goes quiet. Yren is tired, so very tired. They lay on their back staring up into the sun. The light is bright, too bright. Yren needs to sleep. Someone hovering over Yren, staring down, backlit by the sun. They are tall, lean. Weird shadows, like wings, six wings, extend from their shoulders. The wings block out the sun. A hand, outstretched...

The first thing Yren noticed upon waking was how cool and smooth the floor was against their cheek. They're senses registered the smell of metal, the smell of dirt. Yren's body lay flat on the ground, unmoving, but everything around them was swaying gently. It was disorientating. It made Yren's stomach turn. Moving. They were moving! Yren gasped and sat up swiftly, terrified. It was dark and it took a few moments for Yren's eyes to adjust.

"You're alright! It's alright." The voice was high-pitched and unfamiliar. "No one here is going to hurt you, you're safe."

Augi whimpered.

"Augi!" Yren threw their arms around their sibling who was sitting next to them. "Augi, where's Story? What happened to Story?" Yren looked around wildly in the dark. They seemed to be inside a large steel box, not so very different from the Longhouse back home. But they were moving steadily, bumping along the uneven terrain. A little light and a bit of air crept in through some vents that ran the length of the top-most corners of the structure. Filthy rags and torn sheets hung from the ceiling, screening off different sections. Metal benches lined the walls. In the low light Yren could just make out the shapes of dozens of people.

"Story?" Uma looked confused.

"The wolf!"

"Was that wolf your—? They put him in a pen and loaded him onto another transport. Don't worry, he was alive still when they did it. Stunned, like the rest of you, but still alive."

Yren tried to get their eyes to focus. "And who are you?"

A round, brown, friendly face emerged from the shadows. "My name is Uma." Yren could see Uma's broad smile and plump cheeks. There were others, many others, huddled there in the dark of the moving transport, but only Ima seemed to pay them any real notice. They all wore the soiled, tattered jumpsuits of the workers. Some slept, clearly exhausted. Some whispered amongst themselves. Others stared blankly at the two strange, wild children.

Yren pulled Augi in closer to them. "And How Do We Call You?"

Uma looked at Yren and Augi with a puzzled look. "I don't understand. I'm... Uma."

Without a second thought, Yren recited the chant. It gave Yren comfort to speak the words aloud, like casting a spell of protection. "The Universe is Love. Love is where your name is safe in the mouths of others. A name is a spell, a prayer. There is power in a name. It reminds us that we are all a part of the Divine, who is all things – male, female, both and neither. The words we choose have power... the words..." Yren awoke from their trance. "I am Yren. When you do not use my name, say they or them. This is Augi."

"When you do not use my name, you can say he or they. How Do We Call You?"

Uma smiled. "She, or her."

Augi and Yren nodded. "Uma? Where are we going?"

"Back to the encampment. On the outskirts of Citizen."

"Citizen? What's Citizen?"

"You've never heard of Citizen?" Uma turned and caught the

eyes of a frail looking, old worker sitting in a heap on the floor behind her. "You see, Father Daoud! I told you so!"

"What's Citizen?" Yren asked again, more urgently.

"It's the last remaining stronghold of man," said the weathered old worker. "Or so we thought. They told us there was no one else out there. They told us that beyond the Clearing, only beasts and disease remained of the Old World. They told us we were alone."

Uma looked excited. "You're from the wilds beyond the Clearing, aren't you? We've heard stories but didn't quite believe... and then a few months ago a man and a woman just washed up out of the mines and –"

Yren's stomach dropped. They couldn't bring themself to ask. Augi spoke up first.

"Were they alive? The man and the woman who washed up out of the mines?"

"Yes. Yes, they were alive. Injured, but alive. His leg was... very bad. They took them both to treat their wounds, to ready them for work. I heard they were put to work in the mines like the rest of us as soon as they were healed."

Yren and Augi both burst into tears. They held one another tightly as wave after wave of emotion washed over them. In a strange way, because Unti had never allowed for the burial rights, the siblings had never allowed themselves to mourn fully. They had always made an effort to conceal their grief, to shove it down beneath the surface. Uma's revelation had suddenly given the siblings permission to grieve outwardly. Something in them both broke wide open. The aching, the despair, the guilt, the shame, the loss, the longing – it all pushed through Yren like a typhoon as they clung to Augi, gasping for breath. It was a release Yren had never expected to receive, a grace they had dared not hope for in their wildest fantasies. And what remained was such unanticipated joy, it felt surreal. *Ama and Aba had survived the accident! Their parents were alive!* Yren's spirit leapt with gratitude, and for the first time since the accident Yren found themselves silently speaking to the Loving Spirit of the Universe. *Thank you*, Yren whispered to themselves. *Thank you.* Yren wiped the tears from Augi's face and then from their own. Then Yren took a deep breath, as their momentary relief mingled now with a new sense of fear, of dread. If Ama and Aba were alive, no force on earth would have kept them from trying to return to the Village, to their children. Of that, Yren was certain. If their parents lived still, they were not safe. They were not free.

"Uma... Do you know where they are now?"

ƎNꓕ ꓘOOK ONƎ

ACKNOWLEDGEMENTS

For loving me through a pandemic; for supporting me in joy and in struggle; for striving for justice in our communities; for teaching me; for clearing the way and forging a path; for creating the networks of mutual aid that kept me alive long enough to complete this novel my sincerest thanks go out to:

Alex Chichelli
Kristopher Librera
Safia Siad
Ravyn Ariah Wngz
Sly Sarkisova
Griffin Epstein
Thania Vega
Catherine Hernandez
Sarah Pinder
Shaista Latif
Dainty Smith
Milo Ramirez
Michiko Bown-Kai

And for their efforts in bringing my vision to tangible reality in these pages I would like to thank my illustrator, Sydney Kuhne; editor, S. Bear Bergman; art director, kd diamond; and the rest of the team at Flamingo Rampant.